Train Flight

The Birth Of Salvation

ELIZABETH NEWTON

Order this book online at www.trafford.com
or email orders@trafford.com

Most Trafford titles are also available at major online book retailers.

All scriptures are taken from the Holy Bible.

Printed in the United States of America.

ISBN: 978-1-4669-2152-8 (sc)
ISBN: 978-1-4669-2157-3 (e)

Trafford rev. 03/27/2012

 www.trafford.com

North America & international
toll-free: 1 888 232 4444 (USA & Canada)
phone: 250 383 6864 ♦ fax: 812 355 4082

Note:

This story is the second of the Train Flight series. It can be read by itself, but it is also part of the ongoing adventures of Evie and Paulo in the Train with the Captain.

Others in the series so far:

Moon Man

For J.

Contents

Chapter One

Time Crash

"You can't leave me here!" Mallory said, raging with anger. He'd even thought of picking up the chair and throwing it at his companion—or soon to be *not* his companion—but he would probably have been zapped out of existence for doing so.

"I do whatever I feel like doing," he laughed.

"But we're partners!" Mallory pleaded.

"We *were* partners. I fancy flying solo from now on. No offence old chum." He'd said it with no trace of feeling. It had more harshness than the pounding and humming of the machine, which was grinding louder and louder beside him in the gloomy underground chamber.

Mallory had never dared to raise his voice like this to him before. "But I've helped you in the past! I've been your right-hand man! I knew you were a ruthless man, but to do this to *me*?!!"

"Mallory, you've known all along that this invention of mine can only take one person. And it was always going to be me wasn't it," he said, smugly and selfishly. "It would take years to prepare it again for another journey.

Years that I'm not prepared to waste. So I suppose this is goodbye. It has been fun, old friend."

"I'm no friend of yours!"

"So long!" And the man was gone. As if the stifled air in the room had swallowed him up.

Mallory swore at the empty space before him. He threw the chair and shouted again and again at it, straining his throat and causing the veins in his head to bulge with hot blood. Just when he thought his tantrum was over, he turned around and punched the stone wall beside him, wincing in pain and regret afterwards.

He was angry beyond all control and description. He'd never learnt to operate the machine himself and having damaged part of the machine with the chair, he'd ruined any slim chances of getting out of there now.

He was stuck, in a very permanent way. And that was that. But he never came to any settling, contented acceptance of this. And how could he have done, when he didn't belong there? Here in the middle of his prime, his life was over.

*   *   *

8 years later . . .

In the spaceless realm of the time vortex, the Captain and his crew were in trouble. There had been a thud from the Train's mechanics. Usually, a gentle thud was normal after taking off, but this thud had sent the three travellers buckling to the floor of the strange, little spacecraft, and there had been a lot of turbulence following.

"Meteor shower?" suggested Paulo, just as he was tossed violently to one side on the floor.♣

"Collision with another satellite?" shouted Evie Bamford, hoping desperately that it wasn't.♦

"Can't be either of those things!" said the Captain of the Train over all the noise. "The radar screen says there's nothing surrounding the outer hull of the Train!" The Captain was trying to control the Train from the engine room floor. One hand was holding on for dear life, and the other was fiddling with the controls on the central control panel, which at this moment was straight above his head.

But no amount of fiddling did any good. "My controls aren't working!" he told the others. "Nothing I'm doing is making the slightest difference!"

Having come to the conclusion that the controls were locked, the Captain told Evelyn and Paulo to start feeding the Train's furnace with Carnane fuel.♠ "Shovel

---

♣ Paulo Vistar was a young man the Captain had met on a satellite orbiting a planet called Serothia. Although he looked only about seventeen, he was known to be thirty-two years old, but that's only because Serothia rotates around its sun faster than Earth does around *its* sun, so the years on Serothia are much shorter, and so, passing much quicker.

♦ Evelyn was from Australia, Earth, and she had actually been on her way home in the Train, until this sudden emergency had cropped up. She said 'another' satellite because flying fast into a giant approaching satellite was how her last adventure with the Captain had kicked off.

♠ which is just like lumps of coal, only they were already warm, and pulsed a glowing orangey colour. It was especially suited for feeding the Train's furnace.

in as much as you can fit! We need to try and get some thrust from somewhere!"

There was a special stash of Carnane fuel in the floor in between the engine room and the cozy, old fashioned single carriage of the Train.

While Evie and Paulo worked like a machine, shovelling in the coal as fast as they could, the Captain managed to get a reading of the controls. "This makes no sense," he said to himself. "These controls are never wrong!"

"What's it say?" Evie shouted.

"It says we're going back in time. And really, really fast! I can't stop it! 1991, 1973, 1805, 1633, 1211, 321 . . . you'd better get down on the floor, quick! I don't know when this girl's going to stop, but it's certainly going to be a big crash!"

"But the furnace . . ."

"Leave it now, you'll have to!!"

Now every time traveller knows that a time crash is much more dangerous than a physical crash—like something dropping from a great height. So as Evie and Paulo closed and secured the furnace door, the Captain made one last attempt to regain control of his Train. But it was no use. He crouched down on the floor as he'd commanded the others to do, said, "God protect us!" and then waited for the inevitable to happen.

The 'crash' was considerably smoother than he had expected. One could hardly even call it a crash at all. There was a long . . . silent . . . wait.

"Was that it?" said Evie, afraid to open her eyes.

The Captain opened one of his, and glanced around at his all-in-one-piece Train. He opened his other eye and began to get up. Typically, he left Evie in suspense by not replying, and merely looked over the control deck and navigated his hand over all the controls. This was something he did often. If he was blindfolded he would still be able to find every one of the Train's controls just by touch. He'd probably even be able to fly it. Running a hand over the control deck gave him a sort of comfortable feeling. A familiarity. A feeling of being at home.

However, as comfortable as it made him feel—especially so, now that the Train was still in one piece—the controls were still locked. It was just like a computer when it's frozen, only you can't just turn it off and on again.

Evie and Paulo stood up slowly, balancing themselves by walking their hands up the wall.

"Every-everything alright?" asked Evie, timidly.

The Captain just frowned down at his controls.

She tried again, "Captain, what's . . . what's happened?" She waited. Then a smidgen of her timidity vanished. "How come I can hear my voice but no one else can?"

"I can hear you, Evelyn," he said, without looking up, "but technically you shouldn't even be here, so I shouldn't have to be answering your questions."

Evie was hit hard. This Captain that she'd only met a day and a half ago was so unpredictable. One minute, he was really nice and the next, he could seem so cold.

But then he looked up and his eyes met hers. One side of his mouth curled up slightly and he said softly, "I'm sorry. You were going home, and now you're far from it." He paused and then slowly walked around to the other side of the centre control deck to where Evie and Paulo were standing. "You're only fourteen and I was supposed to be taking you home."

Afraid, but trying not to show it, Evie tilted her head slightly to one side and said, "Where are we?"

The Captain, leaning back against the control deck, was plain and straightforward. "We're in the year 4 B.C."

Chapter Two

Angels We Have Heard On High

After taking a glance out of the Train's big front window and checking the scanner for the safety of the atmosphere, the small group of three ventured outside.

"Is it . . . necessary to leave the Train?" asked Paulo.

"Are you kidding?" said Evie. "We're two thousand and . . . fourteen years back in time. This has got to be the most exciting thing that's ever happened to me. Of course it's necessary!" She got a rush of nervous excitement as her foot trod down on the ground from inside the Train. She wasn't even born yet and her foot made an impression in the soft grass. "Hang on," she said, "what planet are we on?"

"Two thousand and fifteen to be precise and it'll make a nice double surprise for Paulo. We're on Earth."

"Earth," Evie said, trying to get her head around it. "Earth, in 4 B.C."

"This is Earth?" asked Paulo—also with nervous excitement, (but a tad more nervous than excited).

"It doesn't look any different from 2011 so far," said Evie.

"Why is it that we can't see your spaceship, Captain?" Paulo asked. He'd wondered that for a long time now, but this had been the first appropriate moment to ask.

"It's the paint," he said.

"It's not invisible," Evie added, "You can actually see its surface."

"The paint causes an optical illusion and your eye sees whatever it expects to see behind the Train. There's nothing but countryside out here and your eyes fill in the big gap where the Train is."

"I know what your next question is," Evie said, with a smile, "and it's because the Captain wears special glasses and sometimes his driving-goggle things, so that he can see it whenever he wants to. It's only through the lenses that you can see it."

"I've never heard of anything so ingenious. The perfect hiding place, anywhere you go."

"It doesn't stop people bumping into it, though."

Paulo smiled, and then tried to refocus on what he was talking about before. "Before, what I meant by 'necessary' though was . . . well . . . could there be anything . . . dangerous around?"

The Captain shook his head quite confidently. "No. Unfortunately. Anyway we're not looking for trouble this time. But a general wander about will be necessary because I need to find out what caused the controls of the Train to lock. And lock onto *this* time and place. And even if I can't find out why, I still need to find out how I can fix it so we can be on our way."

"Well I'm glad we have to wander about," Evie said, starting to stray.

"Ah, remember rule number two?"

"Don't wander off."

"And rule number one, for that matter."

"Stay with you, yes I remember."

"That applies to you too, Paulo. We all stick close, alright?"

"Right," they replied in unison.

"Anyway," added Evie, "it's dead quiet out here in these fields or whatever they are. There can't be anyone around for miles."

"Hello?" called a voice from nearby. "Who goes there?"

The three spun around to face where the voice had come from. They couldn't see anyone at first. *They must be on the other side of the Train,* the Captain thought, bending his upper body over sideways to see beyond it. He saw two men in the dull light of the moon coming up a hill towards them. Towards the Train. He quickly jogged around the Train and stood in front of it to save the approaching men a painful, embarrassing and highly confusing experience.

The Captain heard one of them say to the other, "There. Straight ahead."

The Captain put his hands in his pockets and smiled cordially, "Good evening."

"I thought I heard voices," one of them said.

Evie and Paulo appeared behind the Captain.

Then the same man spoke again. "Only . . . a moment ago, I thought I could see only one of you. Must have been a trick of the moonlight."

"It is very dark tonight, Zac."

"That is true."

The two men had reached the Captain, Evie and Paulo. Evie immediately noticed their clothes. They looked like they were straight out of an old biblical movie.

"What must you be doing all the way out here?" one of them asked.

"Are you shepherds from a neighbouring field?" asked the other one.

Evie was about to answer, but the Captain quickly got in before her (after whispering, "Rule number three.") "Er, well, I suppose you could say that. Yes we are shepherds from a neighbouring field."

The men were clearly looking questionably at Evelyn.

"Oh, this is Evelyn. She was lost . . . way out here and she's trailing along with us until she can find her way home."

"Where are your sheep?"

"Sheep?"

"Your sheep. Where are they?"

Evie wondered whether the Captain was going to be able to whip up some sheep from out of his pocket liked he did with most of his tools and peculiar gadgets. He seemed to be able to whip up a story quite well from out of nowhere.

"They're lost," he said.

"All of them?" the man said with alarm.

"All of them, yes. We'd lost one . . . er, hadn't we, Paulo, and we went to look for it . . . unsuccessfully, and when we came back, all the rest were gone too."

Evie suppressed a chuckle.

"Oh dear. That's awful."

"You'll be out of work for a while, then."

"Yes, yes. That's right. We still have to break the news to our employer, though."

"Are you hungry or anything? We have more than enough for ourselves."

"Actually, we're alright for food for a while."[*]

"I'm Zacchaeus," said the taller man on the left, "and this is Joshua. Why don't you come and rest with us, you won't get far on a dark night like this. We're camping just over the crest of this hill. Continue your journey after day break."

The Captain didn't want to delay his search for whatever it was that could fix his Train but he knew that Zacchaeus was making sense. Someone who knew this countryside well would possibly get somewhere, but being passing travellers, the Captain and his crew would only get themselves lost.

"That's very kind of you, Zacchaeus," the Captain replied, with a gracious smile. "I'm known as the Captain, this is my . . . fellow shepherd, Paulo, and as you know, this is Evelyn."

The five of them started walking down the hill.

"We are fortunate are we not," said Zacchaeus, "to have a fellow shepherd. I remember when I was a shepherd on my own once. My master was much poorer than the one I have now. I would become *so* lonely. It can be unbearable."

"This is my first job," Joshua said, "so I do not know what that's like."

"May I comment . . ." said Zacchaeus, awkwardly, ". . . your clothes seem very . . . well, they're very strange. I've never seen such a fashion."

---

[*] As it happens, only about twenty minutes ago, the three of them plus another friend called Squirt ate like kings at a very posh 5-star restaurant on Serothia (in 2011). They still felt quite full.

The Captain was wearing loose khaki-brown trousers, a cream coloured shirt and over that, a dull blue knitted vest, with his long dark trench coat over the top. He looked just like a 1920s automobile enthusiast, especially when he wore his driving goggles. Sometimes he even wore a leather cap that covered the ears to match. Evelyn was still wearing her jeans rolled up to just under her knees, long black-and-white striped socks with black-and-white sandshoes. She had her favourite warm hooded jacket on.* Paulo still had on his sky-blue, long sleeve overalls from when he was working on Serothia's Satellite SB-17.

"I suppose we do look rather different, don't we," the Captain said.

Before anymore could be said, the group saw before them a large huddle of sheep.

"There they are," Joshua smiled, introducing the travellers to the sheep. "They're a good flock, they are. Something must have spooked your sheep for them to wander off so far."

"Well it only takes one, doesn't it," the Captain said. "And they all follow. Just like . . . well . . . sheep." A thought then occurred to him. "Tell me, did anything unusual happen here in the last ten minutes or so?"

"Unusual?"

"I don't know . . . something in the air, any sounds, a person maybe, someone lurking around?"

"Trying to work out what it was that frightened your flock away?"

"Something that attracted my Train here, actually," he said quietly.

---

* which had in fact saved her life recently.

"Sorry?"

The Captain told him it was nothing, just as a sudden glow of light suddenly appeared in the sky, and it shone down brightly and hit the grass with its beams. It was so bright, it would have blinded all five of them immediately if they hadn't looked away so quickly. It illuminated the land all around them, and the grass and even their own skin seemed to glow with the clean, white light. With light, you expect there to be heat as well, but this light was like a cool, refreshing breeze. But no matter how wonderful it looked, the five were absolutely terrified. They had crouched low on the ground and were now shielding their eyes and trying to see what it was at the same time. Evelyn's heart was racing and Paulo racked his brain for what it could be. The Captain, on the other hand, had a slight, hair-raising hunch.

All five of them were too frightened to utter a word. The light was like nothing any of them had ever seen before. Soon, when their eyes started to adjust to the bright light, they saw a shape—only *brighter still* than the surrounding light. It was very big and very tall, and the shepherds and the travellers were each shaking like a dry leaf.

The shape was a figure, a man in gleaming clothing. When suddenly he looked down on them, they trembled even more. They felt so puny cowering beneath him, but his face was kind, and when he spoke, his voice was calm and smooth.

"Do not be afraid," he said. "I bring you good news of great joy that will be for all people."

Evie's stomach wrenched upwards and swam around and around, as she vaguely recognised the words this giant was saying.

Paulo and the two shepherds were still trembling and couldn't speak. They could only listen. The Captain, (without rising from the ground) began to straighten up and his mouth dropped open in awe.

"Today in the town of David," the man said, "a Saviour has been born to you; he is Christ the Lord."

The group looked up and kept listening.

"This will be a sign to you: You will find a baby wrapped in cloths and lying in a manger."

Evelyn was now in awe as well and she felt weak all over. "Jesus," she whispered, finding her voice and not physically being able to blink.

Just when Evie thought the huge creature looked right at her, a great company of heavenly figures, (she just knew were angels), appeared behind the first angel and the shepherds had to cover their eyes again because of the radiant light.

Then, the most beautiful sound arose from them as they lifted their hands up to the night sky. They were singing, and the three travellers could hear the words very clearly:

Glory to God in the highest, and on Earth peace to men on whom his favour rests.

Their song was like nothing the shepherds and their new companions had ever heard before. It somehow was like fire and water at the same time. It trickled out of their mouths like a graceful stream, yet it withheld so much power, one got the feeling of something about to erupt.

Then, as quickly as it had all happened, the angels vanished upwards, and the light dimmed until it was once again, a ghostly star-lit hillside. The five of them were paralyzed on the spot for a few moments, speechless.

Then, it was Joshua who broke the silence. "Let's go to Bethlehem and see this thing that's happened, that the Lord has told us about."

"The lord?" said Paulo. "What lord? How do you know who brought you this message?"

Zacchaeus answered, "Because it could be nothing else. Have you never heard of the God of Israel? God of Abraham, Isaac and Jacob?"

Paulo had a blank look on his face, and then he glanced at the Captain.

The Captain said to him on the quiet, "This is who I've been telling you about. The Ancient of Days, the One you wanted to meet. The whole reason why you came with me." The Captain then said, more so to himself, "What a perfect time for us to land in, to show you who He is."

"Quickly, let's go," Joshua said. "I don't want to wait. The angel said it was a Saviour that's been born! The Christ, he said!"

"That means he's the Anointed One," said Zacchaeus. "We've heard prophesies about this. This could be the time the prophet Isaiah was talking about." He was already rounding up all the sheep and collecting up their bedding and food supplies. Then he picked up some of their spare clothing, which was amongst the bedding. "Here," Zacchaeus said to the Captain, "put these on, then you'll blend in more, look like one of us. You can come with us."

"What?" Evie blurted out suddenly. "And see the baby?"

"Of course, that's where we're going. And right away. There's no time to lose."

"How far is Bethlehem from here?" asked Paulo.

"Only a few miles west," said Zacchaeus. "We could be there in an hour or so."

Evie was slipping a heavy robe over her shoulders, while muttering to herself, heart still racing, "I can't believe this. This can't be happening. I must be dreaming." She saw that the Captain had just put on his shepherd's robe and was helping Zacchaeus and Joshua gather up the sheep. Evie went up to him and her side touched his, "Is this really going to happen?" she asked softly.

He smiled. He could tell she was as nervous as anything—just like him. His face beamed. "I can't believe it either, but I think it is."

She looked up at him with her young, innocent eyes, "I'm going to see Jesus."

"Right, everyone ready?" Zacchaeus said.

"It's amazing that light didn't frighten off the sheep," Joshua was saying.

"Well the Lord would not want us to lose our job now, would he?" Zacchaeus smiled.

"I hope they won't mind us leaving a whole flock of sheep nearby."

"I'm sure they won't," said the Captain. "There'll probably be a lot of animals around as it is."

"What makes you say that?"

"Well . . . the angel said we'd find the baby in a manger. Well that's what animals eat out of. Maybe they're in some kind of stable." The Captain had had a lot of practice at being careful what he said when he was in the past. For Zacchaeus and Joshua, there was no such thing as Christmas yet. There was no such song as *'Away In A Manger'* here. He didn't have to tell Evie to be careful. When he looked down at her face, he could tell she was already thinking the same thing.

"Why do you think we've been called to see the baby?" said Joshua.

"Maybe so that we can spread the news afterwards. The Lord does many strange things so that He will receive due glory."

Joshua nodded slowly. "I feel so honoured. I mean, if this is the Messiah . . ."

". . . Which we have just been told he is."

"Well . . . we may be the first ones to bow down to him."

The others pondered this and Evie just shook her head in disbelief. *Can this happen?* She asked herself. *Isn't this against the laws of time or something. I don't exist yet, but I'm going to be present at the infamous Nativity Scene. That's in the Bible! How can I be in the Bible! I wonder if it'll get rewritten to say there was a girl among the shepherds. Or will I be classed as one of the shepherds? This can't actually be happening.*

"Are you alright, Evelyn," the Captain said suddenly. They had been walking a while, and she was looking quite tired and had fallen behind the others a little. He fell into step beside her.

"Yes," she said lightly. "Everything's alright 'cause this is just a dream. I'm just dreaming. I must have fallen asleep on the Train. Or even in James' car on the way to Summer Camp✣. And the whole 'Captain-and-Train'

✣　James was Evie's older brother. Before Evie met the Captain, she was with James and a friend called Lisa and they were driving out in the country at night on their way to James' thing is a dream too. The whole lot. That makes more sense actually."

The Captain merely let the corner of his mouth curl up slightly. Not because he was laughing at her on the inside or anything like that. It was because it had crossed his mind that he was dreaming also. *Evie* knew how *he* felt. Then he said, "Are you sure you're alright?"

She looked up at him and bashfully shook her head. After a pause, she said, "Well, I'm going to be a shepherd. I'm one of the shepherds, in the Bible, I'm one of them."

The Captain smiled, "I know. Crazy isn't it."

"I suppose you do this stuff all the time."

"Ah-ah, not this," he shook his head, "This is as amazing for me as it is for you."

"But shouldn't I be feeling honoured or something? Privileged and blessed to be chosen?" She dramatised her words a little.

The Captain's eyes wandered this way and that, "Mmm yes," he said, "Don't you?"

"Well, it's heaps amazing and everything but . . . oh how do I describe it? . . . it'll be like I'm an imposter."

"I know what you mean. But if this wasn't in God's will, I don't believe it'd be happening. He's always got everything under control."

"Na, that's not really what I meant. I mean . . . well . . ."

Just then, the Almighty gave the Captain understanding of what Evelyn meant. "Do you know Jesus? Personally I mean." he asked.

---

youth groups' Summer Camp held at Point Turton, which is across the other side of the Peninsula from Adelaide.

Without looking up, she shyly shook her head. "Well I do, of course I do," she said, "But I don't know . . . I don't know everything about him."

"Neither do I."

"No, but I mean, I don't know exactly . . . why he had to die, and I don't really understand why he's so important and stuff."

The Captain gave a nod and looked ahead at where he was going.

Evie continued, "And like . . . the way he died, all what happened . . . or in our case, what's going to happen . . . it's like, well . . . people in my life keep ramming this story down my throat, but I don't see how I fit in. Like . . . what it's got to do with *me*."

"Feels like more of a story than real life?"

She thought, "Yeah, I guess."

The Captain nodded slowly and pensively. And silently, in his mind he prayed for her.

After a short pause, Evie narrowed her eyes and smiled slightly. "Did you just pray for me?"

He raised his eyebrows and looked back at her innocently.

She laughed, "I've got people back at church praying for me. Praying that I accept Jesus for myself and everything. I guess it can't do me any harm."

He smiled. "Come on, let's catch up with the others."

They quickened their pace and fell into step just behind them.

"Stray one," Zacchaeus said to Joshua and Joshua immediately knew what to do. He broke away from the small group and went over to one of the sheep that had started to wander off to the right of the flock. He put his arms out wide and sidestepped around it, sometimes clapping his hands together and taking hold of its woolly back, until the sheep trying to be individual, trotted over to join the rest again.

Joshua came back with news. "Hey, just over this crest and east a little are a few lights."

"That would be Bethlehem," Zacchaeus said.

"No, they're nearer than Bethlehem. Looks like there is a house there and an inn."

"We will see if we can rest there for a short while," said Zacchaeus.

"They might know something about the baby too. They might be able to assist us."

Paulo moved closer to the Captain and asked in a hushed voice, "Why are we remaining with these shepherds and looking for a baby? Aren't we supposed to be working out what brought us here?"

"Patience, Paulo. Just wait and see."

"Yes, it *is* an inn," Zacchaeus said as they'd reached the peak of the hill. "I'm longing to rest my feet, even if it is just for a few minutes."

Joshua asked if they even had enough money. "An inn is a bit high class for mere shepherds is it not? And we would have to take turns sitting with the sheep outside."

The Captain reached into one of his many pockets and brought out some pieces of silver. "I've got some money here if you need it. But I have a strange feeling they'll be full."

"The inn? Full?" said Zacchaeus. "Surely not this inn, so set apart from the city. They'd get very little business out here I would imagine."

"Sorry, there's no room," said the inn-keeper.

Evie quickly covered up a smile with her hand.

"Look, I know we look poor, we are merely shepherds, but we *can* pay you," said Zacchaeus. "And it's only just for a few moments, maybe a refreshment."

"It's not that sir, it's just that we're all full up, not a room in sight, not a bare space to 'ang yer sandals, no place to rest yer 'ead, no room to swing a cat, we're up to our necks in paying guests! I had to turn away a young lady earlier—great with child she was, and I mean *great*, just a few hours ago. Do you think I wanted to do that? I'd give you the roof but there's a man up there with his three wives and his dog. Gave the last room to a foreigner. Tall, skinny guy he was."

"A young lady with a child in her womb?" said Joshua.

"Yes, with her husband I assumed. They desperately needed somewhere. I reckon she could've given birth at any minute."

"Which way did they go?" asked Zacchaeus.

"Well the only thing I could do was to let them stay in my stable 'round the back. I didn't 'ave the heart to send 'em away." Then he said, "Oh but I wouldn't disturb them if I were you, they probably want a bit-a privacy. Where are you going?"

With no more talking, the five shepherds proceeded along the path indicated by the inn-keeper. It stretched along the road for about twenty metres and then wound back and around behind some trees and shrubs. They led the sheep with them wherever they went until they saw a small barn with a dull light glowing from within. And they stopped. There was a soft mild breeze, and the air was silent, well away from the sounds of the small town nearby.

Wow, the Captain thought. *Wonder Of Wonders.*

"This must be the place," said Joshua.

"This is what the prophets have spoken of for hundreds of years."

"Shall we go and see?" said the Captain, and they all approached the stable, forgetting all about the sheep.

When the stable door was tugged open, two people from within looked up at the disturbance. One was a man with dusty robes and a thick brown beard, and the other was a girl leaning over an animal trough filled with straw and cloth—a manger—with a little baby nestled in the middle, asleep. Then they knew, that this was the place.

Neither Evie nor the Captain could believe their eyes and they were struck dumb with nervous excitement. *

Then the Captain came up beside Paulo who was at the back of the pack now, and made sure he had a full view of the sleeping bundle. He put his hands in his pockets and said, "Paulo, I'd like to introduce you to my Friend who I've been telling you about. The One you wanted to meet. The Beginning and the End. The Comforter and Commander. Creator of all things."

Paulo stared ahead at a tiny helpless baby, and was bemused and speechless.

---

* This was a rare occurrence for the Captain, for he had seen many weird and wonderful things in his life so far. He'd often managed to be amazed, but not struck dumb with nervous excitement.

Chapter Three

Come Adore On Bended Knee

"Forgive us," said Zacchaeus softly, "but we've come to see the baby. We were told by an angel of the Lord that He is the Saviour and this is where we would find him."

"He's wrapped in cloths and lying in a manger and everything," said Joshua, "Just like the angel said."

The man and the woman glanced at each other with a knowing smile and then the man held out an arm and said, "Then by all means, come in. Come and see."

They sheepishly shuffled forward into the open part of the barn, lowering their hoods and fixing their eyes on the sleeping baby.

The woman stood up (with some help from her companion) and smiled at them. "I'm Mary," she said in a kind and quiet voice, "and this is Joseph. It is such a blessed thing that you've come."

"The angel told us that he is Christ the Lord," said Joshua. "But how can this be so? Is a child going to deliver us from the Romans?"

"It is true," Mary replied, "An angel came to me as well and said that He will be the Son of the Most High and it has happened the way it was said to me. Because nothing is impossible with God."

The shepherds, awestruck, fell to their knees, knowing in their heart of hearts that this was the Messiah they had been watching and waiting for. The Captain and Evelyn were among them, but Paulo knelt down just so that he wasn't the only one standing.

As Mary spoke, she was gleaming with a happiness that Evelyn couldn't yet fathom. Her face was radiant, it was clear that her heart was just burning within her. But what surprised Evelyn the most, was that Mary didn't look much older than herself. When she looked at her, Evie saw a face that could quite easily be one of her friends from school.

Joshua was still trying to comprehend what he had seen. "But a child," he said softly—almost in a whisper. "This is not what I was expecting. I thought perhaps some of the prophesies about a baby were metaphors."

The Captain said, just as though it was a passing thought, "Children grow up."

"And the prophet Isaiah said that the Messiah would have humble beginnings and that he wouldn't look like a king,"* said Zacchaeus, noticing that he perhaps wasn't the most beautiful baby he'd ever seen.

"Who is here?" said Mary all of a sudden.

Evelyn's stomach jumped when she realised that Mary was looking straight at her. Their eyes met.

"Why, you're a girl," Mary said softy and curiously. "Why are you amongst these shepherds?"

---

* It says in Isaiah's book, chapter 53 and verse 2: "He grew up before him like a tender shoot, and like a root out of dry ground. He had no beauty or majesty to attract us to him, nothing in his appearance that we should desire him."

Zacchaeus replied, "She was lost, and these two shepherds Joshua and I are with were helping her find her way back home."

When Mary looked at Evelyn, she saw a face that could easily have been one of her friends in Nazareth and when Evie smiled back at her, she saw a similarity between them. Something in Evie's mind somehow expected to see a halo over Mary's head or some kind of glow of light, but this was just an ordinary girl, no different from herself.✤ She glanced down at the Baby and then back at Mary. "You must be such a blessed woman, or . . . whatever it is you say."

Mary laughed a little. "I'm just a servant of the Lord, nothing more. And for some strange unknown reason, He's chosen me to look after Jesus while He's on Earth." She then had a sad thoughtfulness about her and she said much quieter, "Only I cannot imagine the day that He is taken away from me."

Joseph put a hand on Mary's shoulder.

Evie looked back at the manger, "I can't believe it's Him."

"Would you like to hold Him?"

The blood drained from Evie's face as she looked up at Mary again. "What?"

"You can if you like."

"But . . . he'll . . . wake up, won't he? I don't want to disturb his sleep."

"He's waking up now, anyway."

She looked, and the little Baby's eyelids were slowly blinking open. Evie had to catch her breath and her heart felt like it had just skipped a beat.

✤   Back in biblical days, women tended to be engaged to a man at a very young age.

"Here," Mary said, scooping up the little baby Jesus—his arms uncontrollably jerking in front of him like babies' arms do. She leaned in closer to Evie and encouraged her, "Go on."

Evie glanced around to the Captain with a worried, questioning look. She had no idea—it might have ripped a hole in the fabric of time and space if she was to touch this baby. Something drastic like that often happened in the science fiction novels she'd loved reading before she met the Captain.

But he just gave her the tiniest nod and closed his eyes calmly.

Evie looked back at Mary who was holding the baby out in front of her. So she prepared her arms to make the shape of a cradle and Mary placed the precious bundle there. Evie lost her breath again, and she felt her eyes immediately swell up with hot tears. She was looking down on the Baby and the Baby was looking up at her—so helpless and dependant on the support of her arms. She considered again that this was a dream, and she whispered His name under her breath to try and get the situation to sink in. "Jesus. This is Jesus." She gasped and sniffed and laughed and cried. She could not control her behaviour. Then finally, a tear escaped her eye and dropped down onto Jesus' cheek and in that moment, a scripture from the Bible that she had heard in church just the week before came to her mind. If it had not reached her then, it surely reached her now.

He carried our sorrows.

Soon, He started getting restless and His face changed into a frown. Within seconds, Jesus was crying and Evie gasped softly and then smiled and said, "I think He wants mummy."

Mary smiled as Evie handed Him back and she nursed Him.

Evie felt weak all over. She didn't get her full strength back for quite some time. Morning was breaking, and the Captain, Paulo, Evie, Zacchaeus and Joshua had been able to get about two hours sleep in a field near the inn before the sun was up. They counted all the sheep and arrived at the right number.

As she woke, Evelyn asked the Captain to verify that the events during the night had really happened.

"So where will they go now?" Evie asked referring to Mary, Joseph and Jesus.

"Well according to Matthew's gospel, they go to Egypt, obeying what an angel tells them to do in a dream. But Luke's gospel doesn't say anything about Egypt. The next thing Luke recorded after Jesus' birth, was that they go to Jerusalem to have Him officially named and dedicated."

"What's with the gospels all being different?" asked Evie. "That's part of the reason why I find some things hard to believe. It's like they can't get their story straight."

"If you went on a holiday with some friends, and then each of you wrote an account of what happened, wouldn't each of you have a different version? Wouldn't you all remember different things about the trip and have different, individual memories? If you had all written exactly the same thing, I would start to suspect that you didn't go on holiday at all and that you'd planned it amongst yourselves to make up the whole story."

"What do you speak of?" Zacchaeus asked.

"Oh, nothing," said Evie. "What are *we* going to do now, Captain?"

"Well, Paulo and I need to journey back to our master to explain what's happened. And along the way, we need to get you home."

Evie inwardly sighed. She wanted to know what they were really going to do next, but they wouldn't be able to discuss that in front of the two shepherds.

"And as soon as we've taken these sheep home," said Joshua, "we're going to tell our friends what's happened. I can't wait. I'm going to tell everyone I come into contact with!"

"So will you, I hope," said Zacchaeus to Paulo and the Captain.

"Believe me, I'm always trying," replied the Captain. "Well let's get started on our journey, then."

They all headed off in the same direction, but soon, Joshua and Zacchaeus had to part from them. They said their goodbyes and the Captain thanked them very much for being kind and hospitable and allowing them to journey with them. The shepherds had been just about leaping with joy that morning—their faces beaming with wonder and excitement. The Captain and crew were the same, however, Paulo was a little confused.

"The Train shouldn't be far away now," said the Captain after they had been walking a fair way. He put on his piloting goggles that allowed his eyes to see the Train. "In fact," he said with some uncertainty, "I should be able to see it." He looked around in all directions.

"Well maybe it's still a bit further," said Evie.

"Normally I would not believe this comment and say you're wrong, but I'm prepared to give you a chance. Let's walk across these hills for a while longer."

They did so, the Captain leaving on the goggles. But with every step, he grew more and more uncertain.

There was no Train in sight. "We definitely didn't come this far."

"So what are you suggesting? That we took a wrong turn?"

"No," replied the Captain, staring at a patch of flattened grass about a metre away from them. "I'm suggesting that the Train has been moved."

The others followed the Captain's gaze and realised what he was looking at. The flattened grass area was exactly the same size and shape as the Train. It was evident that it had once stood here. But as Evie walked freely over the area, she knew without a doubt that the Train was gone.

Chapter Four

The Familiar Stranger

"I'm sorry," Evie said, "usually I'd be a bit concerned about the fact that the Train is missing, but I just held baby Jesus in my arms and witnessed the first Christmas so . . . there is no surprise that could top that at the moment. I can't think about anything else."

"May I remind you that the Train is your transport home," said the Captain.

"I know. But at the moment I can't contain anything else inside my head. Captain?"

"Yes?"

"I think I understand a bit more about Jesus' death and what it meant and everything."

"Really?" the Captain said, suddenly interested in Evie. "What?"

"Captain," Paulo interrupted, "what are we going to do without the Train?"

"Well it'll be around here somewhere. We're not *without* it, we've just . . . misplaced it."

"How can you misplace something that is, one: quite large, and two: invisible?"

The Captain thought for a second. "Actually, it's very easy to misplace something that's invisible."

"You know what I mean."

"Yes I do," he smiled. "And I don't have the answer at the moment but in order to find it, we'll need . . ."

"A compass?" said Evie.

"A map?" said Paulo.

"A change of clothes," said the Captain. "Come along." He started walking back the way they had come.

"Where are we going?" asked Evie.

"To Bethlehem. Since Zacchaeus and Joshua took back their spare clothes, we once again, look rather conspicuous."♣

"But that's all the way back to that inn and *further!*" cried Evie.

"The walk will do us all good."

"But we've just *walked* heaps already!"

"Of course, we could always use this," said the Captain holding up a gadget that looked like a TV remote control with a blue light radiating from it. "My Atom Relocating Molecular Teleport Device."

"You're kidding?"

"But I only use that for emergencies."

Evie and Paulo were jogging to try and keep up. "You can teleport?"

"Only once every twenty-four hours. That's why it's reserved for emergency situations. Remember, I used it to get from the bridge of the satellite back to the Train in a way that the big blue blob monster wouldn't be able to follow me."

"So that's how you popped up from out of nowhere," said Evie.

♣   which means, they looked like chicko rolls in a bowl of fruit.

"But why every twenty-four hours?" Paulo asked. From his job as a maintenance worker on Satellite SB-17, he'd gained a lot of interest in interesting technologies.

"Once it's been used, it takes a full twenty-four hours to recharge again. Teleportation uses a lot of power. Of course if I was a real *hip* and up-with-the-times kind of person, perhaps like a ghalepathon or a fifty-first century Yaron Model-3 Robot, I'd have a better one. But I'm just me."

"You know," said Evie, "every time we ask you a question to resolve a mystery, you only go and open your mouth and create another mystery."

"Oh sorry, I didn't realise. That's not on purpose."

The travellers had reached the edge of the city of Bethlehem, and Evelyn was absolutely exhausted.

"Can we see if that inn's got a vacancy now?" she said leaning her hands on her knees and panting loudly. "My feet are killing me. I don't think I've walked so far in my life."

"How are you holding up, Paulo?" asked the Captain, his gaze fixed on the city streets before them.

"Fine," he said.

"Yeah, alright, rub it in. I'm not very fit, okay. I admit it." She rested her hands on her hips and looked ahead. "So what are we going to do now that we're here?"

"I don't know exactly," replied the Captain. "Hopefully we'll see something out of the ordinary."

"Do you expect to see something out of the ordinary?" asked Paulo.

"Well first, you need a little knowledge about this time and culture, my man. In 4 B.C., there wasn't a lot of high tech equipment. To be more precise, none. Just *equipment* would be a better word. No computers, no mechanical transport, no electricity. Not in the form you would recognize it anyway. So to be able to move the Train from its place—something very heavy and impossible to see with the naked eye, an object completely foreign to anyone from this time or place—there would *have* to be something out of the ordinary somewhere."

"Let's hope it's in Bethlehem," said Evie.

"Well it's a good start because it's the nearest town. The shortest distance away from where the Train landed."

"Still can't believe I'm in Bethlehem," Evie said. "In 4 B.C."

"Well," said the Captain, "let's get in there! That's history straight ahead of us. Let's go and see it!"

"Alright!" Evie skipped ahead, energy suddenly found again within her. The Captain let her lead the way, but there was no way he was going to take his eyes off her. He could not leave Paulo's side either, for Paulo knew nothing about Biblical times on Earth and he was likely to ask someone the time on their iStream network.

As Evie walked along one of the dusty roads entering Bethlehem, she could hardly find the opportunity to blink her eyes. It was a busy street—probably the market. If she were in Adelaide in 2011 it would have been Rundle Mall. To her right, she was passing a man with a big stomach selling bread loaves to any passers by. To her left, there was a woman choosing between two live chickens and about to give another man some money for one. Then she saw a young boy running towards her down the road, with a plump woman running after him, ordering him to come back. Evie suddenly smelt fish and to her right now was a tall man behind a stall with crates of fish, trying to entice her into buying some.

"Fresh out of the Mediterranean! Top quality! You won't find any that's better!"

She realised he was talking to her and she had to shake her head to indicate that she wasn't interested.

"How much for the blue and orange stripes?" she heard a woman say near her.

"Only three shekels."

"Did you make it?"

"My mother did."

Evie called to the others and waved her arm to bring them over. "You can buy clothes here," she said when they were beside her. "Is three shekels expensive?"

"That's quite good actually," said the Captain. He started looking through all the handmade garments. There were robes, shirts, tunics, and head dresses made of densely woven fabric in all sorts of different colours.

"I'll take it please," said the buyer.

"A good choice," said the woman selling.

The buyer handed over some pieces of shiny metal, took the blue and orange robe and draped it over her shoulder. "You could have charged four," she said with a kind smile, "it is good quality." Then she walked away.

Then the woman selling, looked at the three travellers and smiled broadly. "Large robes for four shekels?"

The Captain smiled and conversed with her without hesitation, starting with a lighthearted joke. "If only I'd arrived before that woman."

She laughed.

He continued feeling the well made garments and looking through all the different colours. "Well?" he said looking over to Evie and Paulo. "Which ones do you like best?" Then he addressed the woman. "Are all the robes the same price?"

"Four shekels each."

"Alright, I'll take three."

"Certainly. That will be twelve shekels."

He looked at some pieces of silver in his hand. "Make it thirteen?"

"Thirteen?"

"Alright, alright, make it a round fifteen. Could you do them for me for fifteen?"

"But sir, it is *I* who am selling them to *you*."

"How about sixteen?"

Paulo whispered to Evie, "What is he doing?"

"He's haggling . . . but he's going the wrong way, you're supposed to try and go *down* in price, not up."

"I'll take seventeen if you want me to, sir."

"Tell you what, seventeen is a bit of a funny odd number. It would make me happy if it was just a round twenty."

"I cannot take that from you, sir."

"Oh please. Go on. Surely you can stretch to twenty."

". . . Well if you insist."

"Of course I do, Evie, Paulo, have you decided?"

"Er . . . yes, I think so . . ."

"Splendid. Here's your silver, and please thank your remarkable mother for providing us with these garments. God be with you."

"How much money have you *got*?" Evie said as they were walking away.

"Oh I'm a, bit of a collector."

The travellers put on their new clothes and Evie felt immediately too hot, but she kept plodding along with Paulo behind the Captain. She found it very difficult to keep moving at this pace because there was always something to look at.

"Excuse me," said a voice nearby. It was soft, kind, and female. And it took a few moments for the group to realise it was them who the lady was addressing.

"Me?" said the Captain.

"I think so," she replied timidly. "Are you called the Captain? And are these not your friends Paulo and Evelyn?"

The Captain glanced at them both with a curious frown. Evelyn felt reluctant to answer, for it may have been some kind of trap. She suspected the Captain felt the same way, but Paulo suddenly spoke up and said, "Yes, that is us."*

Evelyn suddenly felt fearful. "How do you know who we are?" she asked, not being able to stop herself. She remembered that the Captain was supposed to do all the talking. He already had one passenger who had forgotten the rule.

"Forgive me," the young woman said, "but my brother described you to me, and you do look rather conspicuous."

"What? Even with these new threads on?" said the Captain.

The woman looked down at their feet. One pair of shiny brown enclosed shoes, one pair of black lace-up boots, and one pair of worn black and white sandshoes. "I've never seen such manner of foot ware. I knew it had to be you."

"Who is your brother?"

---

*   Of all three of them, Paulo was the most trusting. His home planet consisted of very kind and peaceful people and it was rare for someone to lie and cheat and deceive.

"The shepherd, Zacchaeus. He came to the house through the night and told me about what you had seen in the stable, and he told me that if I saw you in the market, I must be sure to make myself known to you and offer you my home for food and rest."

The Captain smiled. "Did he really?"

"He knew that you might have been in need of guidance, he didn't seem to think that you were familiar with Bethlehem."

"And he was right. We do need a host to show us around. We're becoming a bit lost, I think," he said, speaking for the others as well, placing his hands inside his pockets.

"What do you search for?" the woman said.

"Something very important," he replied, suddenly serious. "But first thing's first, what is the name of our extremely kind host?"

She still seemed shy, but she placed a hand on her chest, "I'm called Rachel. And I will be glad to help you with whatever you are looking for. Why don't you come to the house for refreshment?"

"We'd love to."

And the three followed her straight away. The Captain turned around to his companions, "I knew that young Zach was a good bloke!"

Chapter Five

Bethlehem Blues

When they arrived at a house a few streets away, it was much quieter. There was no hustle anywhere, and not even trace of a bustle. Rachel had some of her own shopping to put inside the house, and just as they reached the doorway, she said, "Please, make yourselves at home."

The house was surprisingly cool inside and very homely, yet there was a dry, dusty smell in the air because the floor was nothing but firm, packed earth. The ceiling was not very high, in fact it was only about a foot above the Captain's head. There were timber beams spanning across the ceiling and it looked like reeds and straw that were laid above them. The windows were small and high up near the ceiling. The room wasn't very big, but what made it homely was that it was cluttered with shelves carrying pots, bowls and spices, a wooden table with bowls of fruit and a basket of fresh vegetables on it and wooden stools beside it.

Rachel dumped her things down on the table. "Do go through and relax, I shall pour some water."

The Captain, Evie and Paulo walked through a low, stone doorway into the next room, the same size. On the floor there was a large rug laid out and lots of lots of cushions propped against the far wall and in the middle of the room, a low wooden table with a pottery jug on it.

The Captain walked straight to the cushions and sat on the rug. "Ahh, luxury."

"Well I *would* get you a refreshment," they could hear Rachel say from the other room, "if I could find the water jug."

"Is this it?" Evie said, picking up the jug on the table and taking it to Rachel in the first room.

"Yes. Thank you."

Just then, an old, large man with a big smile came in through the outside door. "Ah Rachel, you're back. I hope you have something for my hunger."

"I will have, father, but you'll have to wait."

They hugged and kissed each other on the cheek before Rachel introduced her visitors to Elisha, her father. *
Then Rachel said, "You should meet my mother too, she's around here somewhere." She called out, "Mother, Miriam, Jared! Come and meet our guests."

Within seconds, out came an older woman with graying hair and hunched shoulders with two young children at either side of her—a boy and a girl. The boy looked about twelve years old and the girl looked about seven. "This is my mother and two of my children Jared, and Miriam. Mother, where is Joshua?"

"Just got him to sleep. Surely you don't want me to wake him."

---

* It looks like a girl's name, I know. But if you say it as if rhyming it with 'nicer', then you'll know how the boy's version of the name is pronounced. In case you're one for forgetfulness, you could say 'there's no one nicer, than Elisha.' (Coincidentally, this was quite true of Rachel's dad.)

"No, of course not." Rachel addressed the visitors. "Joshua is my youngest boy. He is only six months old and the most beautiful baby you'll ever see!"

"What about us?" said the children.

"He is *one* of the most beautiful babies I've ever seen," she corrected, tickling Jared and Miriam. "I named Joshua after . . ."

"Zacchaeus' friend?" Evie guessed.

"No, after the man of God who defeated the city of Jericho. The one that is spoken of in the scriptures."

"Oh, *that* Joshua," said Evie. She'd learnt about Joshua way back in Sunday School, about how he got an army to march around the city of Jericho and when they played their trumpets, the walls came tumbling down. She then got the song stuck in her head.

"What an amazing God we have. And now, the times are exciting. Zacchaeus said that the Saviour has come. The One who will deliver us from the Romans."

"I wouldn't hold your breath on that one," said the Captain, under his breath.

"Well, here is your water," said Rachel, happily. "I will now start on breakfast."

"I'll give you a hand, Rachel," said her mother.

The Captain stood up suddenly, "You don't have to cook us breakfast as well!"

"I insist!" said Rachel, and that was that.

After breakfast, Rachel and her father were sitting down with the three guests and the Captain was trying to explain what he was looking for, for they were all eager to help.

"Well it's kind of a . . ." he began, "It's made of . . . it's from . . . and it's like a . . . well it's also kind of my mode of transport."

"A horse?"

"A chariot?"

"A camel?"

"No, it's . . . none of those things . . ." he said awkwardly.

"It's kind of hard to describe," said Evie.

"Very difficult," said Paulo. "It's even hard to see it, let alone describe it."

The Captain decided to start using a different tact. "Has anything strange at all happened recently around these parts?"

"Strange?" said Elisha.

"Unusual. Have you noticed anything unusual going on? Someone lurking or, a strange feeling even, that . . . something was different? Something wasn't right?"

He was looking at two blank faces staring back at him.

"Nothing that I can think of, how about you, father?"

"Well, tax has stayed the same over the last few weeks. That's unusual. Usually it goes up. But I gather that's not the kind of thing you had in mind."

The Captain knew that it was hopeless here. He wasn't going to find the answers he was looking for. Not with these kind people. He would have to go looking on his own. How could he ask for help from people who hadn't even seen a train, let alone an invisible, time-travelling, space-explorer train?

All day, he tried to get away, but Rachel's family wouldn't hear of it. They were being far too kind. And as it got later and later in the day, Rachel insisted that they meet her husband who would be coming back from his work in the fields soon.

They ate lunch and supper with them as well. Although they weren't the richest people in the city, they surely had to be the most generous. At some stage in the day, Rachel showed them her littlest boy, Joshua. And when he woke up, they all had a turn holding him. Evie spent some time with all three children. She had in the past thought of becoming a child care worker in life because of how well she seemed to relate with children.

Evie was having a brilliant day. She got along so well with Rachel and her children. But she could tell that the Captain, although just as comfortable as *she* felt, was getting restless and frustrated. How would they ever get the Train back at this rate? Paulo was a little anxious too and he wished that they could spend time in this lovely home care-free, rather than having to worry about the Train.

It was growing dark outside and Noam, Rachel's husband came home just in time to eat supper. It was clear that he adored his children and his wife and her family. And just like the others had already, he embraced the guests warmly and offered them beds for the night. The Captain started to think that they would have to stay there, because they wouldn't get far in their search at night time.

But just then, in a silent moment after a little light-hearted joke and laughter, they thought they heard a scream. A very very distant scream—barely audible.

They all waited in silence to try and hear it again. For a while it didn't come, and so the family returned to their happy conversation. But then, there was another scream, a little closer. Noam and the Captain jumped up off the floor and ran to the door, listening intently to the sounds on the breeze. There were some more screams and then some faint sounds of clopping horses and the rickety wheels of chariots.

"What is it, Noam," said Rachel, standing up.

"I don't know. Sounds like chariots. Have we paid all our taxes this month?"

"We are in no debt."

Elisha got up too and walked through the doorway, standing by the road to see if he could see anything. Noam joined him and Evie walked up to join the Captain.

"There are voices too," said Noam, frowning. "Distressed voices."

The sounds were very slowly getting louder, a little more frequent, and there were more and more voices which spread through the village like a fast-growing virus. There were women's screams and some shouting from men. The sound of the chariots was growing nearer and lamps in houses nearby were being lit and moving about. Other people were coming out to see what was happening and their faces were growing more and more fearful as the screams grew louder. Most of the screams turned into cries and all-too-quick, the sound of weeping was crawling through the town of Bethlehem.

But it was the next sound that wrenched at Evie's heart. It was distant, but unmistakable. It was the sound of a baby crying out. A sound that made something in her mind click, as she remembered something else she'd learned in Sunday School.

"Captain . . ." she said weakly, "Why was it that . . . Mary and Joseph were warned in a dream to go to Egypt?"

His face said it all, showed that Evie's worst suspicions were right. "They had to escape," he said, not taking his eyes off the direction of the sounds.

Evie felt herself shaking and dread drained the blood from her face. "Escape . . . what?"

"The Romans," he said with restrained anger. "The massacre of the innocents."

They heard another baby cry out and a woman, presumably its mother, pleading and crying, and then another scream.

Evie suddenly exploded into action. "Rachel!! Where's Joshua?"

"He's asleep in the crib, why?"

"The Romans are coming."

"How do you know it's the Romans?"

"Who else could it be, Rachel?" her mother said.

"But we have done nothing wrong . . ."

"The Romans don't need an excuse to be brutal," said the Captain coming back into the room.

"You have to hide Joshua!" Evie said.

"*Hide* him?"

"Yes!"

"I will protect *all* of my children!"

"But they're after Joshua!"

"Why on earth would they be after Joshua? He's a baby."

"That's just the point!"

"Evie," said the Captain, authoritatively, "you can't change a fixed point in history."

"I'm not, I'm trying to save one baby!"

"What are you talking about?" Rachel demanded.

Then Elisha came running in from the yard, with terror written on his face. "It's the Romans," he said, disturbed and choked up, "They're killing all the babies."

"What?" said Rachel, breathlessly.

"A new baby was born last night and you know who He is," said the Captain to Rachel with urgency.

"The Saviour," she said, staring into space.

"A new King the prophets say," said Noam.

"And King Herod* isn't going to want any other king growing up and overthrowing his kingdom is he?"

"But my son is not he!" Rachel said, becoming terrified and weak. "They may rest assured that Joshua is not the child Herod is afraid of!"

"They won't settle for that," said the Captain, sadly.

They heard the screaming and wailing outside becoming denser and there was shouting from the Roman soldiers as people tried to resist and disobey them. Rachel recognised the voice of her friend who lived across the road. She too had a small boy.

Evie turned to Rachel, desperately, "Quick, where can you hide him?"

Rachel went and picked up Joshua from the crib.

Noam said, "But there's been a census,◆ Rachel. If you hide, with Joshua, they'll wonder where you are. They'll know we're being dishonest."

"What will we do?" pleaded Rachel, tears starting to well up in her eyes.

"Give him to me," said Evie. "I'm not in the census. There might be a chance."

So Rachel did. But Evie had no idea where to hide.

---

*   who was the king of Jerusalem at this time.

◆   which meant all people in all cities and villages were counted and a record of them kept with the government.

"Go into the courtyard,"* Rachel's mother said. "There's a big chest where we keep linen, but it's empty, for the linen is still in the washing. Go, go!"

"Evelyn," said the Captain.

Her eyes met his. They were sad.

"Don't even breathe or they'll find you."

She left the room with the little six month old bundle in her arms.

"They're coming," cried Paulo, and the remaining party scurried back to the eating-room and pretended—nervously—that everything was normal. Two Roman soldiers burst through the door.

Evelyn pulled her second leg inside the chest and lowered herself so that she could close the top. The inky blackness was unnerving. She heard a tiny sound from the baby.

"Where are your children?" one of the soldiers demanded.

Rachel stood up inquiringly and Jared and Miriam ducked behind her legs.

The second soldier strode over to them and tore them away from her.

"Th-th-these are my children."

"And you will not lay a hand on them!" said Noam, boldly.

"You dare to speak to the king's soldier this way?" asked the Roman and Noam was struck down off his feet by him. The children screamed.

Evelyn could hear the voices and she was sweating buckets. Joshua was waking up, she could feel it. He was

---

*   which is an outside room within the house's outer walls that many houses had in this time.

squirming in her arms and she tried to rock him back to sleep.

"These children are too old," said one soldier to the other. "Let's move on to the next house."

"You are Noam, son of Joab the farmer, are you not?"

"Yes I am."

"It is known you have two sons."

He swallowed hard, "Two *children*, that is. A son, and a daughter."

"If you lie . . ." he placed his right hand on the handle of his sword, which was for now, tucked away in the sheath. "Search the house," he ordered the second soldier.

It was not working. Joshua was awake and the darkness all around was beginning to worry him. He could not smell his mother, and there were strange sounds all around him. Evie tried to lull him by making the quietest calming hums and shushes. But suddenly, very quietly, his little distressed voice broke the silence.

The soldier had searched through the bedroom quarters and found nothing. But he did find the crib and some baby clothes lying around. He happened to also see Rachel and Noam's faces while he was searching. Rachel was shaking and trying to hold back her tears, while Noam's nervous eyes were betraying him.

The soldier became angry as he stepped out onto the courtyard.

Evie tried covering Joshua's little mouth, but was petrified of smothering the poor little thing. All was deadly silent in the house. Everything was still and there was not one sound.

Except, for the muffled crying of a baby.

The searching soldier looked straight to the chest in the courtyard, and Rachel and Noam rushed to him and fell on their knees.

It was not a pleasant sight at all. Rachel was beside herself in fear and sorrow, pleading at the soldier's feet to spare the life of her boy. He wasted no time in opening the chest and with a passionate anger, he grabbed Evelyn out of there and tore the baby from her grasp. Now there was both Rachel and Evie begging on their knees. But the soldier paid no attention to them. He stomped towards the outer door muttering something about *orders being orders.* Rachel tried to steal Joshua from his thick, cruel arms—veins like cables—but she could not disrupt his course. He was unmovable. When the two soldiers were by the door, they hesitated no longer.

I won't illustrate the scene for you, for it is too horrible to put onto paper. But what happened next is extremely vital to the story, so I must pick up there. The first soldier looked directly at Evelyn with a condemning glare. He pointed to her and said, "You have shown contempt against the decree of your ruler, King Herod! For this, you shall be punished."

She looked straight at the Captain and he was, as of now, thinking of a way to get her out of this.

"Bring her!" he ordered his fellow soldier.

Then everyone was saying something all at once.

The Captain said, "You can't take her away!"

Noam said, "Take me instead! I deserve the punishment, not her! I lied to you about my son!"

Elisha was saying, "You, you, you, unspeakable . . . brutes!"

Paulo was saying, "How can you punish someone for protecting a child?"

Rachel was speechless, but hardly silent. Her whole body was jerking violently as she sobbed into her mother's shoulder.

Evie was calling out to the Captain, "Don't let them take me! Captain! Captain!"

They were dragging her further and further away from the house and the Captain was running after them, yelling, "It's alright! I'm right behind you!" But soon, they pulled her up onto their chariot and within seconds, the horses galloped away and they were gone, as quickly as they had come.

Chapter Six

Capture

It was an awful mess. The Captain and Paulo wanted
nothing more than to help Rachel and Noam in this
terrible time but they had to get after Evelyn. The
Captain knew how cruel the Romans could be. Anything
could happen to her. In fact, the Captain was surprised
they hadn't killed her on the spot.

He and Paulo looked across and saw Rachel—
absolutely weak and helpless with despair.

"Why?" she whimpered. "Why?"

"There must be no king but Herod," the Captain
replied gravely, staring into the air in front of him.
He started to feel his own eyes swell up, taken by the
overwhelming sadness in the room, which just moments
before, was filled with joyful laughter.

Paulo did not like this world. Serothian history books
were nothing like this. He did not know how to react,
but he knew right now that he felt absolutely miserable.

The Captain happened to catch Elisha's eye and the
latter came over slowly—sadness marring his face.

"You must go and find your friend, if you can," he
said softly, hardly able to speak. "Don't wait here on our
account."

"I'm so sorry," said Paulo, with the same sadness hanging over him.

The Captain simply put his hand on the shoulder of Elisha, and without having to say anything, Elisha showed them that he was grateful for their attempt to help, and similarly, the Captain let it be known that he was grateful, on behalf also of Paulo and Evelyn of their generous hospitality throughout the day.

And then it was okay for them both to leave.

The Captain had already decided in his heart that they would come back and visit this family again before moving on . . . if they were ever going to be able to move on.

"How did the king know about Jesus?" Paulo asked when they were already a little way down the road.

"Apparently, a group of very wise, learned astronomers discovered the birth of the 'New King' by watching the sky. And because they wanted to pay homage to Him they went straight to King Herod because they assumed he'd know where the New King was. So it was them that made Herod aware of it." He then said, more to himself, "Obviously that's already happened."

"But what of Jesus? Won't he have been killed just like the rest?"

"No. By now, Mary and Joseph and the Baby should be on their way to Egypt."

"So Herod *did* know where he was? And Jesus might not be safe!"

"Relax, Paulo. There's no way the Creator of those stars up there would let something dreadful happen to Jesus." He then frowned to himself, "Definitely not yet anyway." In a new breath, he said, "So, what do you think by the way?"

"Of what? This barbarous world? Not much, if I'm honest."

"I mean what do you think of my Friend? The Beginning and the End. The Comforter and Commander. Creator of . . ."

"The baby? Well . . . first of all, I don't quite get it. And secondly . . . well . . . innocent babies have died because of him. Already. And he's what, only a day old?"

The Captain said softly and calmly, "Many will suffer for His sake. And many will die because of His name."

"What does that mean?"

"This is hopeless," the Captain suddenly stopped. "We're not going to get anywhere fast like this. Jerusalem is about six miles north of here. We need transport."

"I haven't seen any cars around. Not since we got here."

"A car isn't quite what I had in mind," the Captain replied. He had just been looking around the dark village streets for anything they could use to speed up their pursuit of Evelyn, when he'd spotted a friendly face emerging from a dark alley.

Paulo followed his eye-line and saw Elisha coming from the shadows towards them, a horse walking along each side of him—their reins in his hands.

"A thought occurred to me," said Elisha.

The Captain smiled and joined him, taking the reigns from him.

"Now you have an excuse to come back and visit us."

"I didn't need an excuse," he said patting Elisha on the back. "But we do need these horses. Thank you, thank you, thank you."

"May God be with you," he said and farewelled them both with a kiss in traditional Jewish style.

"I must admit," said Paulo. "The Bethlehem people are awfully nice."

The Captain smiled warmly. "Now. Ever ridden one of these?"

"Ah . . . no."

". . . Right," he said coming around behind Paulo. "We don't have much time, so you'll have to learn fast. Any objections?"

Paulo shook his head vigorously.

"Good. Put your left foot in there, the stirrup."

Paulo made a couple of attempts and then said, "Could you hold it still while I get my foot in?"

The Captain did so and Paulo raised his foot up into it. "Now what?" he said, with one leg bent up high, almost tearing his blue overalls.

"Now, use that leg to push yourself up and swing your right leg around to the other side of the horse."

". . . What?"

"Here, I'll give you a boost."

"Sorry, I'm slowing you down."

"No, no. You're alright." The Captain heaved as Paulo lifted himself up, leaning on the horse's back. "Now, swing! . . . and sit! You've got it."

"Well, that wasn't so difficult."

"You're lucky Elisha didn't give us two camels, it would have taken us about ten times as long to do that."

"Now . . . how do I ride it?"

"Give him a little squeeze on his sides with your legs."

Paulo did so. Nothing happened.

"Um . . . squeeze a bit harder, perhaps."

Nothing happened. The horse just changed his footing and kept on chewing on the bit in his mouth.

"Maybe they're not fully trained yet," the Captain thought to himself. "Give him a little slap on the rump, perhaps. Just a tap."

The horse didn't even twitch.

"A bit harder?"

Paulo gave him a whack and the horse took off, spooked as anything. Paulo and his new friend were just a blur.

The Captain called after him, "See, there's nothing to it!" and he suddenly snapped into action himself, put his left foot in the stirrup of his own horse, swung his leg around and got moving at a fast pace after him. And the two horses were galloping fiercely off into the night. Out of Bethlehem.

Evie felt like all of her insides had been shaken up like the contents of a high speed blender from the bumpy ride in the Roman soldiers' chariot. The path had been the worst dirt road you could imagine, and there was no suspension whatsoever in this particular model of vehicle. She did not even have the luxury of being able to hold on, for they had her wrists tangled up in chains that one of them was holding onto tightly. Her bottom had never felt so sore. She was still alive though. She held on to that positive. And when she reflected on the fact that she'd only known the Captain for about two days now and already felt close to death numerous times, she realised how amazing it actually was to still be alive.

It had been a long journey* and although the Romans' destination was not where she wanted to be, she was

---

* If Evelyn was writing this story, she would probably say that 'long' was not a strong enough word. To use her words:

relieved to have finally arrived there. But where was she, exactly? She had no idea. All she knew was that in the eerie dull light of the moon, she could see a giant, ominous shape in the darkness and just as her eyes were beginning to adjust and she could make out that it was a big, tall, majestic looking building, she was pushed harshly off the end of the chariot. She was about to stand herself up to the best of her ability with sore wrists and rear end, but to her disgust and dismay, the soldiers walked ahead of her briskly before she could do so. As a result she was literally dragged along the dry, rocky ground. Being a girl, she thought of her new garment, which the Captain had just bought her. It was going to make a fantastic souvenir from her travels, but now it was ruined. A sharp jab of a stone in her middle made her then realise she was going to come out of this with some serious bruises. A sharp stone tore at her jeans and other smaller rocks underneath her were clawing mercilessly at her stomach and legs, causing her constant pain. She thought her back might be a little more hardy, so she rolled over so that she was being dragged backwards. Clouds of dust were in her wake and her legs were thrashing at the ground. She tried to dig her heels into the dirt, not really knowing what it would achieve. Perhaps she could at least try and stand up. But the Romans kept tugging at her chains, pulling her along, not giving her a chance to get on her feet.

"It had been a loooooooooooooooooooooooooooooooooooooooooooooo ooooooooooooooooooooooooooooooooooooooooooooooooooooooooooooo ooooooooooooooooooooooooooooooooooooooooooooooooooooooooooooo ooooooooooooooooooooooooooooooooooooooooooooooooooooooooooooo ooooooooooooooooooooooooooooooooooooooooooooooooooooooooong, unbearably horrific and bumpy journey that almost killed me."

She was being dragged through a big opening in the building's outer wall, into a vast, sheltered courtyard. Then in through another smaller doorway, there was finally some light. It was coming from the flaming torches perched on the walls.

Then she heard a voice. She wished she could see ahead, but she could find no more strength to be able to roll herself back over again.

"We wish to approach the king," said one of the soldiers. "We have returned from our duty and we also wish to request his advice."

"Go in," said another voice, a little further away.

In the brief break, she was able to get up onto her feet, so when the soldiers pulled her further along the now-stone floor, she tried to stay close behind them so she wouldn't stumble back down again.

The lighting was bright in this next room and she was finally able to have a good look around. But now that she could, she didn't much like what she saw. The room was large and open with fat pillars of stone spaced evenly about. There were deep red and purple drapes hanging from above windows and to conceal other parts of the room and the drapes were bunched and held together with gold tassels and jewels. But it was what was straight ahead, that poured the fear into her. The soldiers were leading her to a sort of podium in the very middle of the room. On it, a throne. And on the throne, a large man with a thick groomed beard, dressed in elaborate red robes, wearing gold necklaces and chunky rings. A king. *Surely*, Evie thought to herself, *it's King Herod*—another character she had heard lots about in the Bible. Only up until now, he'd been just a character in a story. Not a real person. But there he was. In the flesh. Large as life. Larger than the average human being anyway—he looked like he could have applied for *The Biggest Loser: Bible Times Edition.* He had cold, harsh eyes and when they shifted suddenly onto Evie's eyes, she felt her stomach jump up into her mouth. In her primary school years, King Herod was portrayed to her as a villain, and so without having to think, she immediately loathed him and thought of him as her enemy. She thought for a moment that she should give him the benefit of the doubt, but then she remembered that he'd just ordered all the baby boys in Bethlehem to be killed.

"Who is this reckless girl you bring to me?" he said. His voice was smooth, but throaty and glutinous, as though he was trying to speak and swallow at the same time. The hardness in his voice, Evie guessed, matched his heart.

"A Bethlehem girl," one of the soldiers replied. "She attempted to hinder us from fulfilling our orders, showing outright rebellion to the law. We wanted to know what you want done with her."

Herod inclined his head to one side as he looked at her. Evie felt extremely uncomfortable. Every inch of her was being inspected by his stare and she wanted to run away there and then.

"She is a mess. A tangled mess of a thing, but . . . I'm glad you kept her alive, I may have some use for her."

Without being able to stop, Evie suddenly burst out, "But I can't stay here. All I was doing was trying to save my friend's little innocent baby! How cruel can someone be to do such a thing! Joshua wasn't the new king you were looking for!"

"What do you know of this *new king*?" He sat forward in his seat with an angry, suspicious face. His dark eyes narrowed. He had a lazy eye which was now just a slit, and the other one was shining with malice as he peered at her from it. As well as all this, Evie could almost smell his foul breath.

Realising she'd said something she shouldn't have, Evie was silenced and she looked down at the floor bashfully. "Nothing. I don't know anything really. Just . . . heard stuff."

He remained there for a few seconds, with rage in his face, and murder on his mind, but then he sat back, turned up his nose and growled, "Aah, take her away, I don't want her. I don't wish her to be my problem. Lucius," he addressed one of the soldiers, "you said your household in the barracks is struggling. Take her to your home and make her one of your slaves."

Evie looked up, "But . . ."

"Get out of here and count yourself lucky you will have a roof over your head. Take her away," he said to the soldiers.

They tipped their upper bodies to him, turned a 180 and marched out of there. Evie was not ready for their brisk departure and so she stumbled again as they pulled her along.

Lucius was the soldier that seemed less superior to the other one. He was the one who received the other's orders and the one who had opened the chest's lid in Rachel's house to find her hiding in there.

There was chatter among the two of them when they came back outside, and then Lucius took Evie's chains in his hands, while the other one took the chariot away. She was alone with Lucius.

She expected him to say something, but he merely started walking again, yanking on her chains and causing her feet to kick up dust and continuously trip over her long, filthy robe. Her wrists were grazed and bruised from the chains. She didn't know whether she'd be able to take much more of this.

Chapter Seven

New Home

This must be Jerusalem, Evie thought. *I'm pretty sure King Herod lived in Jerusalem. Unless I'm wrong about that.* What she wanted was a street sign. Or a petrol station on the side of the road saying, "Jerusalem Petrol Station" or "Jerusalem Convenience Store". But that was unlikely to happen, seeing as there were no cars here to need petrol. Could there be a camel stop with the sign "Jerusalem Camel-Feed Station"? But did it really matter where she was? It occurred to her that it wouldn't make a difference whether she knew or not. What mattered was whether the *Captain* knew where she was. Now *that* would be handy.

The trip with Lucius was not very long. After a short, brisk walk, he came to a stop. They'd arrived at a large cluster of stone houses not far beyond Herod's temple. These were bigger than the houses back in Bethlehem. This, Evelyn guessed, must be where Lucius' home was.

The night was thick, but there were telling signs that dawn was not far away. The sound of the early-morning birds beginning their song for the day, and a unique stirring breeze beginning to spread the word of morning through the leaves in the trees. It made Evelyn realise how tired she was. She'd been on the move all night. It felt good to just stop, never mind a hot bath and a lie down. Lucius started walking again, but it was a slower, calmer walk. He regarded Evelyn next to him, and making sure the chains were still fastened well around her wrists, he loosened them a little, allowing her to keep up without being tugged at. He made a few turns through the narrow streets and finally arrived at the door of a house, which was opened to them.

"You're late," said the woman who had opened the door. "And who's this?"

"We had to ask the king what to do with her. She was disobeying the law. From Bethlehem."

"Why bring her here?"

Why are they speaking in English? Evelyn suddenly thought.

"He said we can have her as a slave."

"We already have one."

"Why do you refuse to have another? There are some who'd give an arm and a leg to have two slaves."

"Never mind, I'll find use for her." The woman looked at Evie. "What is her name?"

"Evie. *My* name's Evie." She felt tired of being talked about as if she wasn't present.

"You'll speak when you're spoken to," said Lucius.

The woman said, "Bring her in, Lucius. Don't have her standing out there in the chill of the night."

Evie felt a glimmer of hope in her heart from these words. This woman sounded nice. Maybe her employers were going to be kind. *Are they called employers when they won't be giving me any pay?* she wondered. *Slaves don't get paid do they?* Evelyn had no idea what to expect.

The woman had walked briskly back into the house, and once Lucius had brought Evie into the first room, he faced her towards him, looked at her and inspected her clothes. He picked up the heavy, dusty fabric of the robe in his hands, shook them and straightened them up a bit. But in the process, the robes came loose and revealed some of her clothes underneath. The left shoulder of her jacket, her sandshoes and a little part of her jeans could be seen. She bit her lip and looked up at Lucius. He had a frown on his face in reaction to these strange garments he'd never seen before. Before he could say anything though, the woman called from another room.

"Bring her here, I want to show her something."

Lucius prodded Evie along towards a kitchen and then into a small passageway. There were some steps downwards, and they led down into an underground room, lighted only by an oil lamp the woman was holding. It shone dull light onto the walls in uneven flickers and made shadows that wriggled unpredictably around the room.

She placed the lamp on the floor and Evie could see now that in the room were two mats laid out on the floor, one of which, she threw a rug onto. "This is where you shall sleep, Evie," said the woman.

Lucius seemed to dismiss himself and walked back up the steps, leaving the two ladies together.

"You may sleep now if you like. You would be tired from the journey. You're no use to us heavy-eyed."

Evie couldn't believe it. Surely this was pretty good treatment for a slave.

"What do I call you?" Evie asked.

She looked at her sternly. "You call me Mistress." Then her face softened. "But my name is Camilla."

"And you're . . . Lucius' wife?" Evie guessed.

"Yes," she said with a slight frown as if to say, *who else would I be?* "There is another slave, whose name is Callista. She will show you around and tell you how to do things."

Camilla started to leave the room.

"Camil . . . I mean, Mistress . . ."

She turned around. "Yes?"

Evie didn't quite know how to say what she wanted to say. "I don't . . . I'm not . . . I mean, I've got friends who are probably looking for me. I don't belong here."

"You broke the law, so you will face the consequences the king decides."

"But, I only tried to save a little baby's life, that's all."

Camilla's expression revealed that she was shocked and wanted to know more about why Evie was being punished. But she simply said, "You cannot take it up with me. It is none of my business."

"But I'm not even from around here!"

"You are from Bethlehem, I know."

"No, I'm from another . . . well, I come from somewhere a *long* way away!"

"Well, now this is your home. Go to sleep Evie. In the morning, you will be more cheerful."

Camilla left the lamp in the room and headed back up the steps.

"I doubt it," Evie said quietly to herself. "How are Paulo and the Captain ever going to find me here?"

She looked around the room and found no sleeping gear anywhere to change into. No tooth brush or tooth paste. And definitely no teddy bear to keep her company like she had at home. She stripped down to her jeans and t-shirt, took her shoes off and slid herself in between the rug and the mat. As she lay in this strange, hard, uncomfortable bed, she missed home more than ever. And no matter how tired she was, it was another two hours before she finally fell asleep.

In the gloom of a downstairs room of another Roman household, Marius' wife called from the bedroom. He sluggishly obeyed, trudging up the narrow, winding steps.

"What on earth are you doing? Come back to bed and get some sleep, Marius."

"When are we expecting our visitors again?" Marius asked, slipping inside the covers.

"Lucius and Camilla are due here tomorrow evening some time."

"Why must they come again? I'm a very busy man."

"Camilla is my sister. They live so far away, him being a king's guard and everything, that I never see her anymore. I don't know why we had to stay in this house when we got married anyway."

"Because I built this house myself, and I cannot leave it."

"Yes I know, I know, because of whatever it is that you've got down in that underground cellar."

"It happens to be very important to me."

"Yes, so important, you don't even allow *me* to go down there. I suppose it's a nice birthday surprise for me or something. And that's why it's so secret. Even though my birthday is months away. I can't imagine what it is. If that's what it is. I hope it's what it is, and not something strange or sinister." She paused. "Marius? Are you listening?"

Marius pretended to be asleep.

Chapter Eight

The Empty Busy Road

There was a pale blue glow of light hovering over the horizon in the eastern sky. Dawn was pushing its way upon the city. As Evelyn admired the beautiful artistry, she yawned broadly and Callista rebuked her.

"I would get out of that habit if I were you, you might easily do it when the master is awake. God help you if he sees you."

"He didn't seem all that bad to me. Besides having to carry out dodgy orders. Anyway, I can't help it if I need to yawn."

"Well don't say I did not warn you."

Earlier that morning, there had been a harsh prodding at Evie's side while she was lying in bed. Someone had been trying to wake her up just as she'd gotten to sleep, saying something like *it's time to get up and start the chores.* She'd opened her eyes allowing a slit of light to seep through her lids and in doing so, saw a young girl leaning over her in a white nighty. This must have been Callista, the other slave Camilla spoke of. She'd gotten to bed even later than Evie and hadn't even been heard . . . until now. Evie had been dreaming it was her mum who was waking her up for school. And when her mum's voice had suddenly fused into the girl's voice, the whole nightmare of Jerusalem came gushing back. Callista seemed alright though. She was eighteen years old and in slavery because her mother and father had been as well. She was not the cheeriest of souls and would certainly not win any prizes for optimism, but Evie felt comfortable around her—free to ask questions.

Now the two girls were out the front of the house, Callista sweeping the stone path around the door, and Evie soaking some clothes in a big wooden bowl under Callista's instructions.

Evie yawned again, this time covering her mouth, hiding it from Callista. "So how come Lucius isn't off to the palace or temple or whatever you call it to work for King Herod this morning? I would have thought their mornings would be pretty early too."

"They are. But he has been given some days of rest. That's why they're heading over to visit her sister today. It's a long trip, so they'll be a few days."

"What do we do when they're gone?" The word 'escape' filled Evie's mind.

"*We* won't be here. People take slaves with them when they go on long trips. It's been me in the past of course. But I'd bet everything I have that they'll take you this time."

"But you're more experienced."

"Yes but you're new. They're not going to trust you here all by yourself. Robberies and runaways happen all the time you know."

"What's that?" Evie suddenly said, looking at the ground near Callista's foot.

"What?" She seemed put out for being distracted from her work.

"That, that just fell out your pocket, pouch thing."

Callista looked down and went to grab it, but Evie beat her to it.

It was a small round silver coin, about 2 centimeters in diameter.

"Never mind what it is. I found it."

"It's pretty." Evie was just about to give it back to her, but something suddenly caught her attention. Something was very wrong with it. She turned it over, and wasn't able to control the change in her face. Her eyes were wide and her brow drew inwards. "How'd you come to have this coin?"

"I found it," Callista said grumpily, snatching it from her and putting it back deep into her belt pouch. "Just found it when I was working, that's all, now leave it, will you?"

"Why are you so cagey about it? I was just curious."

"Cagey?"

"Um . . . secretive."

Callista came nearer and whispered in a harsh rasp, "Why do you think? We slaves have nothing. And that's the way it's meant to be. Or don't you realise that? If I am caught with this, it will be taken from me. And as you said, it is pretty. It is probably worth nothing, but I want to keep it."

There was no immediate response from the confused Evelyn and so Callista returned to her duties.

Evie couldn't leave it at that. "Where exactly did you find it?"

"Oh that's enough, girl! I did not steal it if that's what you're thinking. Now get back to work, before the master comes and sees us chatting."

Evie returned her focus on the clothes she was scrubbing. But in her mind's eye, all she could see was that coin. Something was very wrong here. And she didn't need to be an expert time traveller to know it. It was understandable why Callista would want to keep it to herself, but why would it have the words ONE SHILLING on it? And what on Earth was the face of King George VI doing on it? King George VI was the sovereign of England before Queen Elizabeth II. Coronated in 1937 A.D. In other words, a *long* time after the year 4 B.C.

"Whoa, whoa, whoa! How do I stop this thing again?" Paulo asked, rather urgently.

"Pull on the reins, my friend, and . . ."

Paulo did so immediately and the poor horse came to such an abrupt stop, that its front hooves lifted up off the ground, sending Paulo sliding off its back and into a heap on the dusty ground behind it.

". . . and hold on," finished the Captain, with a slight smile. He rolled his eyes and jumped off the side of his horse. "Now I'll have to get you back on there again."

"Can't we take a short break? My hips are killing me."

"Certainly not!" he replied holding out a hand for Paulo. "It's been a hard day's night, but we can't hesitate for a moment. Every *second* we do, could mean bad news for Evelyn."

"I don't think I've ever felt tireder."

"*More* tired. You've never felt *more tired.* And I know, at this time of day, we should be sleeping like a log, but we must . . ."

"Must find Evelyn first, I know," he said, sincerely.

The Captain helped Paulo onto his horse and this time, it was easier than the first struggle.

"Tireder is a word," Paulo then said.

"Maybe on Serothia, but not here on Earth. Come on, let's keep going." He got up onto his horse again and they trotted up to a road that had not been far away. There was a man on the side of the road standing behind a little stall selling pots, lamps and pottery dishes and all sorts of odd trinkets. Not far behind the road was a big, wide-stretching wall and clear evidence of a big city behind it.

"Is this Jerusalem up ahead, my good man?" the Captain asked the plump man behind the stall.

He confirmed that it was and the Captain gave a broad smile.

"Well, here we are then," the Captain said to Paulo hospitably after they'd passed the merchant.

"What makes you think Evie will be in this town?"

"Because this is not just a town, this is the biggest city in Judea."

"So?"

"Well it's the main city. The capital city if you like. Do you have capital cities on Serothia?"

Paulo hesitated.

"Never mind. A bit of Biblical knowledge allows me to make an educated guess that the Roman soldiers would have brought her here. *This* is where King Herod resides."

"Oh, I see. You think she was taken to the king?"

"Probably. And . . . there's only one way to find out for sure," he said slightly nervously.

"What's that?"

"Go to the king's palace."

". . . Are you sure that's the only way?" Paulo asked feebly.

Surprisingly, the day had gone really fast, what with all the work Evie had to do. Her and Callista had been given a break each to eat and rest, but there was always something to do. The work wasn't particularly hard, just tedious and Lucius and Camilla seemed to be nice enough people. Lucius was a hard man, but still friendly. Evie hadn't seen the strictness in them yet that Callista had kept talking about.

When the sun was low in the sky, Lucius summoned Evie to where he was lounging in what you and I would probably call a living room.

He said, "Soon, we will be ready to begin our journey. You'll need to come with us, and Callista will stay behind."

Evie nodded her comprehension.

"It is a long way from here, so we'll have to make way almost immediately, understand?"

"Yes." Evie understood. But how on Earth was the Captain going to find her if they kept moving her about? She felt all of a sudden like slumping onto one of those cushions herself and putting her head in her hands. She was feeling more and more depressed by the second.

"Well," Lucius said, "go on, and get prepared to leave. My wife will need assistance in packing some of her things."

"May I ask, er, sir, how long you'll be staying there?"

"Of that we are not sure yet. But it can't be longer than a week, because I am due back at the palace in a week."

Evie gave a polite bow (not quite knowing whether this was the done thing) and left the room.

She helped Camilla pack her things into a big canvas sack and all of the stuff got put on a wooden cart with two wheels at the back—a bit like a roofless carriage.

Every time Evie went outside with another item to put on the cart, she gave the road a long stare, wishing that she could see in the distance the Captain and Paulo making their way along the busy streets, searching for her. She would throw down whatever she was carrying into the cart and sprint faster than she'd ever sprinted before over to them and say, "Thank goodness you're here!! I've been made a slave and I was about to be taken to who knows where for a week-long stay. I thought you'd never find me!!" And they'd take her away, the Train will have been found by now, and they could all get out of there!

The street was busy. People doing their last bit of visiting and trading for the day, people coming home from working, people getting their belongings inside before the night approached, but there was no one Evie recognized. No Captain. No Paulo. It was a busy road. But it was empty.

She ached all over. From both the work, and from being lonely and unsure about her fate.

"Come on, we'd better get moving. Is that everything, Evie?" asked Camilla.

"Yes. Everything that you wanted packed is here."

"Let's get moving then," said Lucius, "before the streets get any busier."

Evie didn't even get to say a farewell to Callista, not that she really minded. She would probably have just filled her Evie's head with her grumpy, pessimistic voice. She was a barrel of laughs, that one.

As she hopped onto the cart with Camilla, while Lucius tied on the horses, Evie decided to think about the coin that fell out of Callista's pocket early that morning. How could it have gotten there? All sorts of possibilities whizzed through Evie's mind. All of them seemed unlikely.

It wasn't long before the cart was moving by the efforts of a tired looking horse up the front. Evelyn had felt relieved that it wasn't going to depend on her efforts to tug them along—being a slave and all. She'd never been so thankful in her life, for a horse.

After a long walk for the horses, a difficult time getting passed the Roman guards and many stops to ask for directions, the Captain and Paulo finally found themselves being leered at by a tall and vast palace. Not to mention the Roman soldiers standing like sturdy trees at the entrance. They were without a doubt being leered at by it all—in a rather frightening and leering sort of way.

At least, this was how Paulo was feeling. The Captain, on the other hand, as if totally oblivious to the danger signs, waltzed right up to the nearest soldier.

"Good day, erm, my good man. I'd like to see the king, please."

"You'd like to see the king?" said the Roman, in a mocking, sarcastic sort of way.

"Yes, that's right."

"That would be King Herod, would it?"

"King Herod, yes. Unless there's a team of kings ruling this nation, they failed to put *that* in the history books. It is King Herod I'm after, yes."

Paulo had just reached the Captain's side when the Roman soldier and other soldiers around him started cackling through their noses like naughty school boys.

"Get out of here!" the first one said, "and stop wasting our time."

"Well I . . . I'm not trying to waste your time, I'm being serious here. I wish to speak with the king."

"Well you can't! What are you, mad?"

"No," sniggered the other one, "just really dumb."

"I can speak perfectly well, thank you. Can't you hear my voice?"

"They mean you're stupid, Captain," said Paulo.

"I *beg* your pardon? Tame your tongue!"

"Not me, *I* don't think you're stupid."

"Why is it that I can't speak to the king?" the Captain asked the Roman soldiers.

"Because he's busy."

"Oh you mean I should make an appointment?"

"He won't just speak to a mere civilian."

"Shooting star," said the Captain, more to himself, "when I want to speak to *my* King, I can do it any time of day!"

"Look, just beat it, will you. You're taking up our time!"

"But you'd just be standing there anyway!" said the Captain. "Look, it's about a girl. I believe she was brought here late last night, you might have been here when she arrived."

"We're not interested in your problems."

"Yes, that's the problem with the government, isn't it."

"Her name's Evelyn," said Paulo, quickly, before the Roman could react to what the Captain had said. "She would have been brought here by soldiers just like you."

"Look, just forget it. She's broken the law and so she'll be long gone."

"I didn't say she broke the law."

The soldier shrugged. "I guessed."

Paulo said, "Look, please just tell us what happened to her. Where did she get taken?"

"Young thing with dark hair, right?"

They nodded.

The soldier's face was suddenly sporting a malevolent grin, enough to make a weak stomached person feel a bit sick. The Captain and Paulo suddenly feared the worst. But then, the soldier said in a low gruff voice:

"She was a lucky one. Usually they go and live down in the dungeon for the next twenty years of their life, but this one, Herod didn't want her there. He didn't want her to be his problem, or something like that . . ."

The Captain smiled slightly with his lips pursed, thinking of Evie, the trouble-maker she could be.

"So she ended up as a slave of one of his men," continued the soldier.

"Who? Where?"

"That's enough! The rest is the king's business!"

He was serious. Paulo could tell because even the Captain chose not to push the soldier anymore after that. They shrunk away, with more questions hanging on their lips than they had when they'd arrived. When Paulo looked at the Captain after they were away from the soldier's eye-line, the Captain was beckoning him over to a wooden cart that was parked near the palace wall, filled with hay. He was standing casually behind it, but slightly stooped, as if trying not to be seen. Paulo casually walked over and casually did the same. There they were, casually stooped behind a pile of hay, casually eavesdropping on the Roman soldiers.

"Nothing but a bag of trouble, that girl will be."

The other one laughed. "Yeah, poor Lucius, being stuck with her. Rebellious sort. I've seen them before. She's not slave material."

"She will be by the end of the week."

They laughed together. And that was all that was worth hearing. At least now, the Captain had a name. Lucius.

Chapter Nine

Behind The Closed Door

A whole day gone, and Paulo and the Captain had had no luck. The large community which was still technically within the palace grounds was where they were looking, because this is where respected servants of the king resided. But they'd had no luck yet, because it was so huge. They'd come across one Lucius, but it was the wrong one. There was no Evelyn he knew of.

Their horses' shadows were long tall giants along the dusty ground and the poor things were exhausted. The Captain was feeling weary as well,* but something he saw down the road a little way, suddenly put a sparkle back in his eye and made him spring off of his horse.

Paulo watched him as he jogged down the road. It appeared as though he was pursuing somebody.

He was. Through layers and layers of people, there was one particular head that the Captain thought he recognised the back of. Dark brown hair, almost black, the same colour robe as Evie had bought the day before. Finally! The Captain let out a sigh of relief as he caught

_____

*   which is something he would hardly ever admit to, and it
      was quite a rare sight.

up with her, then stretched out an arm and tapped his hand down on the girl's shoulder. She spun around with a start. And staring back into the Captain's face, was *not* Evelyn. He was looking at a perfect stranger. The word disappointment, would be a terrible understatement. He suddenly remembered his manners. "I do beg your pardon, I thought you were somebody else."

The girl looked older than Evelyn—not nearly as pretty. She gave a polite and shy little nod and kept on walking, leaving the Captain standing still in the middle of a sea of moving people.

Callista looked back at the man who had just tapped her on the shoulder. His face disappeared back into the crowd in a second. The man looked foreign, she'd thought, and he looked saddened and desperate. She shrugged, and hurried to get back home with her basket of shopping.

It was the sudden stop of noise and bumps that woke Evelyn. The sudden calmness and silence disturbed her. Then Camilla's voice beside her said:

"We're here, Evelyn. Get up and help me carry our things indoors."

It took her a while to orientate herself—remember where she was and who she was with. She had a vague sense that she'd just dreamt of home, but she couldn't quite remember anything about it. She got up slowly rubbing her eyes and stretching out her legs. She looked at her surroundings. There was a house ahead that they were walking towards, which was similar to Lucius and Camilla's own house. Only the area was a lot less busy—not only because it was nearly night time, but because they must have been a little way out of the main part of the city. Evie likened it to a quieter suburb like where she lived in Adelaide—not many houses around, and more trees and bushes instead.

A woman emerged from the house, perhaps a little younger than Camilla, with her arms out wide, greeting them.

"Camilla, so good to see you, come here and let me give you a hug!" The two women hugged and then she said, "Marius is not here! We were expecting you later."

"The trip was shorter and easier than we had estimated," explained Lucius.

"No matter. Come in and make yourself at home."

"I'll just get some more bags from the cart."

"Let your slave do that!" she said. "Come in! Have a drink!"

And with that, Evie was left outside by herself.

"Oh for goodness sake!" she said out loud to herself when she was alone. "Do you have to get slaves to do *everything* for you? What lazy so and soes!"

Nevertheless, she trudged all the bags in and asked where they should go.

The evening wasn't too bad after that. They allowed her to settle into the slaves' quarters. It was even smaller than the one at Lucius and Camilla's. She had to bring them drinks and take off their shoes but that was all until bed time. She had to prepare Lucius and Camilla's bedroom for the night, which involved making up the bed, lighting the lamps and unpacking the rest of their belongings.

There didn't appear to be another slave in the house that worked for these people. That is, not until somebody interrupted her little snoop around the place.

"What are you doing?"

She turned around with a start. Before her was a boy of about fifteen or sixteen. Big nose, big lips, dark shadows under his eyes and smooth, rich olive skin. His facial features were arranged in a way that was not unpleasant to look at.

Nervously, Evie answered, "I was just er . . ."

"Snooping?"

"No! I wasn't."

"It looked like it."

"I'm becoming accustomed to my . . . new home. Well it will be for the next few days I think."

"The master doesn't like slaves snooping about. Go back to your duties."

"What's through that door?" Evie asked before she could stop herself.

"That's none of your business," he replied, coldly. Then, his face softened ever so slightly. "In fact, it's none of my business either. No one's allowed down there. Only the master, Marius. So I don't know. Now come on, come away from there."

"What's your name?"

"Levi."

They started walking back away from the closed door Evie had asked about, and then back to the slaves' quarters.

"Is it just Marius and the lady who lives here? Is she his wife?"

"Yes. Her name's Portia."

"Is she nice?"

"Depends what you determine as *nice*."

It didn't sound promising. At least Levi was turning out to be not bad company.

Later that night, while Evie was tossing and turning for the second night in a row, trying to get to sleep, in yet another strange bed, she heard a noise. Turning over and forgetting about it was impossible. She had to know what it was; otherwise she'd have no chance (instead of the current 2% chance) of getting to sleep.

The others in the household were asleep. She could tell by all the heavy, even breathing going on in each part of the house. She could also hear Lucius' snoring which had become familiar to her from the night before. She had wondered how Callista and especially Camilla ever got any sleep.

She supposed they had gotten used to it. And this notion made her suspect that the strange noise she now heard had caused the same effect. The funny thing was that it wasn't a strange noise. Not to *her* at least. But it should have been a strange noise to anyone living in this time. It was the most ordinary noise to Evelyn, but it was like finding something as ordinary as a radio in a deaf person's house.

The noise was a low-pitched hum. If Evie was in her own bed at home, she might guess it was the refrigerator over in the kitchen. She almost didn't give it another thought, until remembering again where she was and *when* she was. She chucked off her blanket and stood bare-footed on the cold, dusty floor. Without thinking twice, she knew where she wanted to look first. The closed door that Levi dragged her away from earlier. It had intrigued her from the moment she saw it. There had been no closed doors at Lucius and Camilla's house. Nor at Noam and Rachel's house. From what she could tell, people in this era and culture had nothing to hide in their houses, and they deliberately left doors open to let the air flow through all the rooms.

After making her way through the house, she was confronted by the door. And she was determined to open it.*

She took one more look around her to check there was no movement in the house, then she reached out and opened it. It wasn't locked. She wondered whether locks had even been invented yet. And she was strangely excited to see before her, a narrow passageway; and evidently a little nervous about the fact that it was leading downwards. Directly at her feet was the first step down. And the steps continued until they disappeared into a deep tunnel of darkness. She could just make out that they curved around a corner a little way down.

Now she was in two minds. To journey down the steps or to try and forget about it? She had determined that whatever the humming sound was, it was coming from the bottom of these cold stone steps. And she thought without a doubt that a little mystery was unfolding. First the shilling, and now the low hum. Pieces of a puzzle?

She had to proceed down those steps. She placed her left foot down onto the top step and immediately, she felt engulfed by the darkness. She made one more step down and then allowed the wooden door to swing shut behind her. Now, it was totally black. She could not see her own feet plodding down on the steps in front of her.

---

* She would have been terribly disappointed if 1.) it was locked, or 2.) all that was behind it was a dustpan and broom and other house cleaning equipment.

She kept putting one foot in front of the other, thinking with every step that she'll surely get in trouble for doing this.

She soon reached the curve, and the steps wound around to the right a little more than 90° and then shortly afterwards, they bent back again towards the left about 45°. The whole time, Evie felt unstable and vulnerable—descending these creepy steps one by one in the darkness and nothing to hold on to but the cold, uneven stone work of the narrow walls.

Evie began to wonder whether there was ever going to be 'a bottom step', or whether she would be climbing downwards further and further until she reached the centre of the earth. If so, how was she ever going to climb up again? And if so, what in the world would be waiting for her at the bottom? And what possible purpose could there be in such a tunnel?"

Just then, the ground underneath her was flat. The next step was at the same level as the last step, and so was the next step and the next step. *Gosh, I've reached the bottom,* she thought, but she could still see nothing but black.

No, hold on, there was a light. One speck of blue light in the corner of her eye. She walked over carefully to where she thought it was situated. The blue dot reminded her of her brother's laptop, and the little light that let him know that although it was in sleep mode, it was still on and ready to function.

Evie only put her finger over the blue dot to try and feel what it was, but that tiny little act seemed to open up a whole troublesome barrel of monkeys. There was a faint *click* and then a low rumble, slightly louder than the hum she could already hear. The next thing that happened was the flicking on of more lights near the original little light and then spanning outwards, flickering on, were thousands of lights, several at a time.

Evie backed up as the lights quickly drew, out of the darkness, a shape. There were green lights now and yellow ones and red ones, and one big area of white light shining. As Evie kept backing up, she realised that the 'thing' she had evidently just turned on, was huge . . . and covered in lights.

It was like a giant computer booting up and she didn't know what to do other than wish with all her inmost being that she hadn't put her finger near that little blue light.

Then there was a buzz and she worried that she'd wake up the house full of people. But all of a sudden, it was quiet again. All except for the low hum that began this little midnight adventure.

What was in front of her is difficult to describe, but it was definitely a machine. And definitely *not* a machine native to this time and place. It looked advanced even for *her* time.*

She recognised individual parts of the machine: a small flat soft-touch keyboard, a few different-sized gauges and exposed wires and things; but as a whole, she'd never seen anything like it before. Above the white-lit area at about eye-level, there was an empty space, bordered by wires, and electronic-looking objects all pointing inwards to the blank space.

Evie stood there staring at it for a good twenty seconds and then after that, she thought to look around at the rest of the room now that she could see it. But there was

---

* Which was the early 21st century.

nothing else in the room. The machine was central and it was the only item in this gloomy underground lair. The room itself reminded Evie of a dungeon because it was cold and dirty, and the walls were a dark grey stone with patches of black—probably charred by torch light.

Her attention came back to the machine. She wanted to turn it off and get out of there, but at the same time, she wanted to find out what it was for. This was not natural. Here she was in 4 B.C. and she was looking at a high-tech piece of machinery that to her knowledge hadn't been invented yet in 2011.

Overwhelmed suddenly by the complexity of it all, she realised she could do nothing to discover the secrets of the machine. But the Captain was sure to know what it meant and what to do. So she decided to turn it off, and if she happened to bump into the Captain again at some time in her life, she would ask him about it.

Having made up her mind, she took a step towards it, but then stopped dead as she realised, this perhaps wasn't her choice to make. Turning it off was much easier imagined than done. The sensor button that she'd pressed by accident to turn it on was a little blue light. But when she looked back at the spot now, it was lost in a myriad of lights. Her stomach jumped. *Now which one was it?* There was no way of telling. It was like playing the game 'Memory' with a pack of cards. You know the match is in that general area, and you *think* it was that one on the left, two spots in from the end, but it could have been three spots in from the end or in the row below it. There was no way of knowing for sure.

Evie panicked, but then told herself to be calm. She was the only one there, she had time to think. She definitely couldn't ask for help.

It's all down to you, she told herself. *Now think. Which one?*

She approached the area with her eyes on the button that her gut feeling was telling her was the right one. And when her finger reached out for it, and she pressed it . . .

The machine whirred into some kind of action—she could tell by the rise in its hum. The great white light shone brighter and there was a chattering deep down in the mechanics of the machine. Suddenly, the blank space hovering above the radiating white light was not blank anymore. Evie's mouth dropped open. The machine had not turned off. She was wrong about the button. Instead, it had created a hologram. All the electronic pointy objects were projecting into the air, an image, and it was this image that caught Evie by surprise.

She stared straight ahead, wide-eyed at the large floating three-dimensional projection, hovering over the strange machine, so vividly.

She muttered in disbelief, "I think I just found the Train."

Chapter Ten

A Little Midnight Gardening

Through the night, Paulo and the Captain were walking their horses wearily. Although Paulo felt like they were also walking aimlessly, the Captain appeared to have some kind of purpose in his step.

"You act like you know exactly where we're going," Paulo commented.

"Do I? Oh, that's good. That's the look I was going for."

"So you *don't* know where we're going?"

"I didn't say that."

"So you do have an idea?"

"I didn't say that either."

Paulo had the most tired expression on his face, and his shoulders drooped in a silent sigh. "Are we actually getting anywhere?" he asked.

"That depends on where we're trying to get to."

"Well, to find Evelyn. Or the Train. Or *both* if we're lucky. Wouldn't it be good if we found Evie *inside* the Train."

"We need to find Lucius."

"But we can't knock on every door in the city. That would take a year at least!"

"What?!"

"Well, maybe not a whole year, but it would definitely take a long long time!"

The Captain had walked quickly ahead leaving Paulo behind with the two horses either side of him.

"Well it *would*!" Paulo said after no response from the Captain.

The Captain waved his hand in the air in Paulo's general direction, while crouching down and looking at the ground. "Yes I know, I know. It was *this* that I said *what?* to."

Paulo walked over and joined him, peering down.

"What? I don't see anything."

"This plant."

"Oh the plant." Paulo squatted down with him. "What about it?"

"Well surely you can see that's it's not native to this . . . oh, of course you can't, I apologise."

"Every plant in this place looks peculiar to me," Paulo said. "So you say it's not supposed to be growing in these parts."

"It's not supposed to be growing on this *planet*," corrected the Captain.

"Really?"

"That is to say, not this world. It's from . . . somewhere else."

"What is it?" said Paulo, reaching out to feel its strange texture, curious as always.

The Captain slapped his hand away fiercely. "Don't touch it!"

"Ouch."

"Sorry about that, but it's deadly. Your finger didn't brush over the top of it did it?"

Paulo shook his head honestly. He had to settle for looking. Its tiny leaves were dark green with a smoky purple tinge and it covered a small patch of ground like short woolly grass.

"I mean, it's not deadly if contact is made with the skin only, but if you bit your nails or ate a sandwich or picked your nose or anything afterwards, you'd be a goner."

"But what's it doing here?"

"That's what I'd like to know. And is this all, or is there more?"

"I wonder if there's been anyone who's touched it."

"Precisely what I've been thinking."

"Could it be related to the disappearance of the Train?"

"Yes, I've thought about that."

"It could be a lead."

"Yes, that's what I think."

"You do think about lots of things at once, don't you."

"That's me. The Thinker. I was the one Musée Rodin got to pose for his infamous sculpture."

"So what do we do now?"

"Well we can't leave this here. We'll have to dig it up. Only, my gardening gloves are in the Train. Drat." The Captain got up from his squat and sat down on a tree stump, one elbow leaning on his lap, his forehead resting on the back of his hand. He looked just like the famous sculpture. "Think, think," he said to himself. Then he stood up and walked back over to the horses.

Hanging on one side of the Captain's horse, was a canvas bag. He tugged it off and handed it to Paulo. Then he found on the ground near a cluster of trees a fallen branch, which he used to start digging up the patch of ground in which the plant was growing.

"We'll need to scoop it up, roots and all, into that bag."

Paulo was about to ask *how*, but he waited and started to think for himself instead.* He remembered he was wearing two sets of clothes. His own blue overalls—uniform from Satellite SB-17—and on top, his Bethlehem 4B.C. robe. He unwrapped himself from the robe the Captain had bought him and used the material as makeshift gardening gloves.

The Captain looked up from his dusty job to wipe away the sweat from his brow. "What are you doing in your overalls?" he exclaimed.

Paulo started his task of scooping with the robe.

"Oh, good thinking," said the Captain and continued digging up the deadly plant.

"This stuff doesn't look all that deadly," said Paulo after a short while.

"Never underestimate the Kratilier Lumis."

"The *what*?"

"That's its scientific name. It's more commonly known as the Violet Assassin."

Paulo could feel himself start to sweat—but not from the work. "Now I believe you," he swallowed.

---

*   Evie had told Paulo during their trip to Bethlehem from the fields that the Captain's rule #4 was to not ask unnecessary questions. He didn't believe there was such a thing as a stupid question, but there was certainly such a thing as an unnecessary question. With just a little thinking or waiting, or doing or praying (whatever that meant), the answer would reveal itself.

A short while later, the two of them straightened up.

"Well," said the Captain wiping his brow again. "That's a good job jobbed."

"Sure we've got all the roots?"

"As sure as I can be."

"It's not dangerous if it's breathed in is it?"

"No. Just consumed. Its native home is a sort of tropical jungle and some animals use it to trick their prey into eating it. When it flowers it looks like fruit, you see. The victim eats the fruit, they wander around a bit and then die. Easy lunch."

"How horrible."

"Fact of life. Only not for us if we accidentally touch this stick or your robe. We'd better burn these when we're done."

"I feel quite nervous with this bag in my hand."

"We'll hang it back on the horse and see if there's any more of it growing about the place."

"How big can it grow?" he asked while hooking the bag onto the horse's saddle.

"Well it starts off looking like a harmless ground cover, but then within five years of its life, it grows upwards and the fruits start ripening. Now *they're* dangerous if you just touch them, but that'll only make you terribly ill, not kill you. I've never actually known how large they can get. End of horticultural lesson, now let's go."

Without waiting another second, the Captain and Paulo both spun around on their heels and there, they froze. They couldn't get any further. Something, or rather some*one* was in their way.

"Paulo," said the Captain, out the corner of his mouth. "Is it just me, or is there a giant, slightly intimidating

Roman solider with impressively large muscle tone standing in front of us?"

"It's just you, Captain. I wouldn't say slightly intimidating, I'd say *very* intimidating."

"You have broken the law," said the tanned and solid Roman.

"Oh hello, I'm the Captain and this is my friend Paulo, how do you do? Now, you say we've broken the law," he looked around. "What is it we're supposed to have done?"

"You have trespassed on private land and destroyed precious vegetation."

"Well I'll give you the trespassing bit, but that there was *not* precious vegetation."

The soldier reiterated, slightly angrier. "You have stolen a portion of the king's property."

"I HAVE *NOT*," he said, feeling his integrity had been damaged.

"What is in that bag, then?"

"That there is *not* the king's property. It shouldn't have even been here in the first place. I'm only doing the king a favour, really."

The Roman's face grew angrier, but he was in control. He took one giant step towards the bag.

"It's deadly that stuff, I'm removing it for you," the Captain said.

The Roman opened the bag with one hand and went to plunge his other hand inside, before Paulo quickly said, "No!" and pulled the Roman's hand away.

The soldier's eyes stabbed Paulo's harshly, "What is this?" he said in a low, gruff, authoritative voice. "Bruttius. Otto." He appeared to be calling to some other soldiers.

Then he looked back at the two gardeners, "You shall be repaid for this."

The Captain smiled, modestly, "Oh, thank you very much, it's really not necessary. Saving people from deadly things is just in a day's work for me."

Paulo whispered, terrified, "I think he means for me grabbing his arm like I did."

Two other Roman soldiers appeared behind the first one.

"Arrest these men. They have disobeyed Roman law and one of them made an attempt to assault me." Before he'd finished barking like a guard dog, Bruttius and Otto had seized them. The men were so strong, the Captain and Paulo had no hope of wriggling out of their clutches.

Then the nameless one said, "Bring them," and at his command, Paulo and the Captain were dragged harshly along the dusty ground away from the scene. Meanwhile, the canvas bag of Violet Assassin was left resting unattended against the horse's side.

Evie lay in bed wide awake, staring into the blackness above her. She had been down in that underground mystery for at least a half an hour before she had decided to climb back up to the house. She'd had no idea of what the time was and so for all she knew, it could have been daylight in five minutes and she would have been discovered. But as it turned out, she had hours to wait in her cold, hard bed. There was no way she could sleep—too much on her mind. *If only I had my book to read to make the time pass quicker*, she thought to herself. The book she was reading at the moment was a blend of fiction and non-fiction called *The Mystery of Space and the Forth Dimension.* But then it occurred to her, *who needs to read up on theory when I'm right here living it out?* She'd been fascinated by space and time travel ever since she saw her dad watching Tom Baker create a time loop with his sonic screwdriver in order to put the destruction of a spaceship on hold, in a re-run of the old '*Doctor Who*'s. She never dreamed that her fantasies of seeing the stars and history books a little closer would become a reality.

After about an hour of mixed up, tangled thoughts, Evie heard a noise in the house. She lifted her head from the pillow to hear clearly. There was someone walking around. It couldn't be Levi because he was sleeping in the same room as her—he'd have heard him get up. It could easily have been any of the others, only, it sounded like someone coming in from outside the house.

The next thing Evie heard made her sit up. It was just footsteps, but they were slowly getting quieter and quieter—as if getting further and further away . . . downwards. Surely, the person, whoever it was, was walking down that long, narrow passage of steps.

Chapter Eleven

The Price To Pay For Prying

The Captain and Paulo had not been very far away from King Herod's palace. It was only a two minute walk until they arrived at the inner courtyard with Bruttius, Otto and the other one—the leader.

The Captain plunged both his hands down deep into his pockets and said, "So, what's going to happen now Bruttius?"

There was no response.

"Otto?"

Again, no answer.

"What's your name by the way?" he asked the other soldier.

"Silius," he said without looking at him.

The Captain looked back at him as if he didn't believe the man. Then he glanced at Paulo, who was right next to him and both of them simultaneously let out an almost silent chuckle.

"Your second name's not *Soddus* is it?"

"You will step inside here," the Roman said, oblivious to their joke.

The Captain nosed in through the door Silius had indicated.

"Doesn't anyone sleep around here?" he said, his voice echoing across a big room, well decorated and furnished, with another Roman soldier at the end behind a brass desk.

"Come forward," the Roman said.

All five of them walked forward together. The three Roman soldiers with Paulo and the Captain removed their golden hats with what looked like bright red broom heads on the top and held them under their arms.

"Do you have anyone to represent you in trial?" the one seated asked them.

"No," replied the Captain, "but it can be arranged if you give me two or three days."

"And you?" he asked Paulo.

"N-n-no," he replied.

"Very well, the trial will commence now. Will you present the crimes com . . ."

"Wait, wait, wait, hold on! I don't have anyone representing me!" said the Captain, "I just said that!"

"The trial must take place at the present time."

"But I said that I could . . ."

"SILENCE!!! What crimes have these men committed?" he asked Silius.

"They were both partaking in the destruction of the king's property."

"Digging up the ground," clarified Bruttius.

"Do you have reasoning for your actions?" he asked Paulo and the Captain.

"Yes," said Paulo. "We were digging up a dangerous plant so that it couldn't harm anyone."

"There is no dangerous vegetation in this area," said the man behind the desk. "This deed will not bring about major punishment. Perhaps they were mistaken about the plant. I will give them a small fine."

"That is not all," said Silius. "The younger one attacked me."

"Attacked you?!" said Paulo, with a disbelieving laugh behind his voice.

"How?"

"He forcedly twisted my arm when I reached into one of their horse's saddle bags."

"That's because the deadly plant was *in* that bag. If you'd have touched it, you'd have been in a lot of trouble!"

"SILENCE! You have already stated that no one is here to represent you, and so you must remain silent."

"Hang about," said the Captain, "in that case, *I'll* represent him!"

"And what have you to say?"

"Well . . . the deadly plant was in that bag and if he'd have touched it, he'd have been in a lot of trouble." He looked at Silius, "If you'd have put your hand in that bag, you could be dead by now!"

"Did you hear that?" said Silius. "The man is making a threat."

"I am not."

"Did you intend to harm this soldier?" the man asked Paulo.

"No. I intended to save his life."

"I do not believe what you say about the deadly plant. And because no lasting harm has been done to my fellow soldier, I will merely issue you a fine."

"Fair enough," said the Captain. "You've been very reasonable. How much?"

"Five Thousand shekels."

"Five thousand shekels, no prob . . . FIVE THOUSAND SHEKELS?!"

"You protest?"

"I can't pay that much!"

"You oppose the law?"

"What I mean to say is that . . . I don't own that much, and therefore I am unable to pay it. If I did have the money, please be assured that I would be most willing to give it to you . . ." then he added quietly, "As long as I knew it was going straight to Caesar where it's meant to go."

"What is it you say?"

"I can't . . . we can't pay that much."

"But you are wealthy, you have fine clothes and even a ring on your finger." He noticed a silver ring around the Captain's pinky.

"Yeah but, that's *why* I don't have any money, because I just spent it all buying these clothes."

"Your ring may suffice. What is its weight?"

The Captain looked up at him. "I can't give you this ring."

"You are *unable* to, or you *won't*?"

"I won't. It has sentimental value."

"So be it," said the man, becoming much angrier.

"Captain," Paulo warned quietly out the corner of his mouth.

"You have made this choice." The man stood up and said one word that Paulo didn't like the sound of at all. "*Banishment*."

The fact that Evelyn woke up when Levi was prodding her, must mean that she fell asleep at some stage. It was time to start the day's work. She always dressed in her

2011 clothes and then put her slave clothes on over the top. If there was ever any opportunity to escape, she'd be ready.

Things were done slightly differently in this household, but there was nothing too difficult or strenuous—just boring, and continuous again.

There was a new voice in the house, one that Evie did not recognise, and soon, she saw the face that went with it.

"That's Marius, the master of the house," Levi explained to Evie in a whisper.

"Portia's husband?"

He nodded. Evie looked at Levi's face, especially his eyes. There was fear there, without a doubt, and Evie was not looking forward to meeting this Marius.

Levi moved on and as Evie watched the little group in the main room about to sit down for breakfast, she noticed Marius was the only one not smiling. He'd sat down opposite his wife and as the lighthearted conversation proceeded, he kept his head down, shoveling in one mouth full of food after the other. His hair was black and cut short, close to his head. He had a thin layer of black ungroomed stubble above his lip, around his mouth and on his chin. He had fat, stubby fingers and wore the usual Roman clothes, but soon, it struck Evie that something was not quite right about him. Something about him screamed 'out of place' but she couldn't for the life of her figure out what it was.

A flush of burning heat rushed to Evie's face when she suddenly realised his eyes had met hers when he'd glanced up momentarily from his plate. In a second, she quickly disappeared from the doorway and got on with her work.

Later that morning, the house was quiet. The hosts were outside in the courtyard at the centre of the house with their guests and Levi was cleaning the roof.* Evie had to sweep all the floors and dust everything while they lounged outside. She gave the closed door, which led to the underground room a glance as she swept past it. She could occasionally hear an eruption of laughter coming from the group outside and she felt like going out there and thrusting the broom into the hands of one of them saying, "Sweep your own dirty house!"

Then she had to stop sweeping for a second because she thought she heard someone coming. Normally she would have kept on sweeping, so that whoever it was could see that she was still working and not getting herself into mischief. But she kept silent this time and ducked out of sight, because the person, whoever it was, was heading towards the 'closed door'. She couldn't let an opportunity like this go past. She *had* to have a snoop to see who it was—even though she already had her suspicions.

She nosed around the corner, and the door to the passageway was just closing behind the person. She quickly tiptoed over and slid her body in through the small gap before the door completely swung shut. It was pitch black apart from a small moving glow of light from deeper within the passageway. Evie followed the torchlight silently, trying to keep her steps in exact timing

---

* Houses in these times and in this area of the world were built with flat rooves so that in the hottest months, people could sleep up there—too hot inside! Also it was easy to build on extra rooms on top if needed. The stairs would be built on the outside wall of the house.

with the torch-bearer's steps so that any noise made by her would go unnoticed.

Suddenly, the light was still, and the footsteps stopped. Evie knew they were no where near the bottom yet. She froze, deadly still—not even daring to breathe. An unbearable silence followed for what felt like minutes, until thankfully, the footsteps started again and the light proceeded down the steps. Evie decided not to take off again so soon. She would create more distance between her and the person in front of her before moving on.

At the bottom section of the passageway there was a curve of the steps, and so Evie was able to hide herself around the corner about ten steps up, while she listened to the sounds that came from the big dungeon-like room. She heard a sound emit from the person—a half sigh, half grunt, and then the sound of the machine booting up. Evie wanted so much to use her eyes as well as her ears and she wondered how far she could lean out before she would be in full view of the person using the machine. She ever-so-slowly leaned her upper body forward, poking her head a little way out into the open. There was still quite a lot of wall, so she placed one foot down onto the next step in front of her and leaned around a fraction more.

She could see the figure, luckily facing the other way, but the person had a long black robe on with a hood covering the head. Like last night, the room was lit up with the many lights of the machine, and the person had hooked their torch up on the wall. Evie looked at the monstrosity. She could tell an image was working its way into the empty space above the white light but she couldn't . . . quiet . . . see . . . what it was . . .

She felt her foot slide off the step she was on and heard the sound of it slapping against the hard stone floor like a clap of thunder. She froze and looked up at the figure. She saw one slight movement of his or her head and didn't wait another moment for it to turn all the way around. She ran up the steps, two at a time, as fast as she could.

Immediately, she could hear running footsteps after her and she didn't care that she was breathing heavily now, almost whimpering. She tripped as her foot missed a step and fell forward, her hands saving her fall. She risked a quick glance behind her, but couldn't see anything. They were about half way up the passageway and her pursuer had not bothered to grab for the torch. The steps in front of her were getting darker and darker until she couldn't see a thing. She tripped again, misjudging the steps in front of her and this time, she landed painfully on her stomach and her voice made an involuntary cry. Next thing, she felt a hand grab onto her ankle. She tried with all her might to yank it free, but it was too strong a grip. She felt herself being pulled back down the steps. She heard herself cry out a second time and as she tried to gather all her strength to break free again, she felt another hand grab her around the waist and then the hand that had yanked at her ankle was now clasped around her arm and she was hauled up off of the ground and back onto her feet—all while she was struggling to get free. She could now sense by the person's strength, that he was a man and he now pulled her in tightly in front of him so that she could no longer use her arms. He dragged her back down the steps this way, while she kicked and protested with her legs. She tried to get a grip on the steps with her feet, but he'd only haul her up off the ground entirely. She was a paper plate in his hands. She had absolutely no control.

When he reached the bottom, he threw her onto the hard floor across the room and then headed straight to the machine to turn it off. Then he leaned over her, a cowering, quivering leaf on the floor and he held the torch between them. She saw now, that it was Marius, as she had guessed. Late thirties, Roman clothes, angry face—but something was not right—*what was it?*

He demanded in an angry, raspy whisper, "What have you been up to? What do you know about this place?"

Evie stuttered, "N-n-nothing, honestly, I don't know anything!"

"You lie!"

"I don't lie. I have no idea what all this is!!" she shouted.

He pushed his hand harshly over her mouth. "You make too much noise and I'll kill you right here on this spot."

Evie looked up at him with unreserved fear. Her eyes started filling up with tears.

"Tell me the truth," he whispered angrily, "why did you follow me down here?" He uncovered her mouth.

She whimpered, "I . . . I . . ."

"What were you doing down here last night?"

"What?"

"Last night! I know you were here! Who are you?"

"I . . . I'm one of Lucius' slaves and I . . . accidentally stumbled across it, that's all. I heard a noise."

"And you thought you'd see what it was, ah? Did it occur to you that you were sticking your nose where it does not belong?!"

She nodded, then quickly shook her head. She didn't know what to say.

"What do you know about this machine?"

"Nothing. Nothing!"

He looked at her in some kind of disgust. Then he pulled at her clothes. "Stand up."

She did so and then wiped her runny nose with the back of her hand.

He looked down at her and the whites of his eyes gleamed in the dim, dreary light. Evie suddenly realised that she was shaking with fear. He had the look of a killer in his eyes.

He said softly but with terrifying authority, "You will forget everything you have seen here and you will *not* come down here again, understand?"

Without hesitating, Evie nodded with passion. But in the back of her mind somewhere, she knew she couldn't forget this and the mystery couldn't stop here. This man knew where the Train was and so really, this was just the beginning.

"We're going back up to the house now," Marius said. "You will *not* speak of or think any more of this. If you do, I will get rid of you."

She nodded again, and they walked up the steps together, in silence.

Chapter Twelve

The Deal

The sun was hot, the ground was dry, and Paulo and the Captain were hungry. It was only mid morning but already, the sun had a harsh bite and the Captain had found it necessary to strip off his B.C. Bethlehem outfit, as well as his jacket and knitted vest that he usually wore. Paulo had his overalls unbuttoned at the top revealing a white T-shirt underneath.

Eventually, Paulo said, "What does one do when one's been banished, Captain?"

"Well . . . I don't know exactly. We live, well . . . we exist. We survive. Someone's decided we're a danger to society and so we've been withdrawn from it."

"What's to stop us going to another city?"

"Some nice weather and some transport."

"But . . . couldn't there be villages out here? There must be someone about."

"Good point Paulo," the Captain nodded, raising his index finger. "I mean, I'm no expert on being banished, it's only ever happened to me once before. But that time I . . . kind of deserved it. But you would think, it being a popular kind of punishment, that there would be others about the place."

"Unless they've all been banished to completely different corners of the planet."

The Captain raised his finger again. "Good point." Then he went into a deep think.

"Where exactly are *we*, Captain?"

The Captain's lips bunched up on one side and he nodded slowly.

"Another good point, Captain?"

"A good *question*. Although we can't be far from Jerusalem. We weren't travelling for long."

"Those blindfolds don't half stink," Paulo said.

"Hello!!" the Captain shouted, with his hands cupped around his mouth.

The sound of his voice was swallowed up by the vast plane of nothingness.

He tried again and this time, Paulo joined in.

After about the twenty-first time, they were sure they heard something far off in the distance.

"Did I imagine that?" asked Paulo.

"No, I heard it too."

The Captain looked around carefully, but there was nothing to be seen. He then licked his index finger and held it up in the air. "Fair bit of wind out here."

"Well it wasn't me," said Paulo.

"Wind's coming from that direction," the Captain pointed forward, ignoring Paulo's comment. So then he walked briskly in a straight line—forward.

"Oh that sort of wind," said Paulo, running after him to catch up.

"Wind carries sound, did you know that, Paulo?"

"Of course I did, Captain."

"Good. So if we heard a sound, but there's nothing around we can *see*, it must simply be too far away to see it."

"That's where the wind comes in."

"Helpful little friend sometimes, wind."

"But I feel like we're heading *away* from Jerusalem."

"We possibly are, but if we're going to get *anywhere*, we'll need help. And a sound, shows promise of help."

"Let's hope so."

That morning, Silius returned to the two men's horses. The obedient things were still standing there, keeping each other company.

Now if there was something Silius had a soft spot for, it was horses, and the first thing he did when he reached them was stroke them gently on the nose and neck and hummed to them softly.

"What am I going to do with you two, eh?"

They nodded at him affectionately and faced their bodies towards him. The bag that was hanging up on one of the harnesses came into Silius' view and he looked at it curiously.

Then he puffed out a breath of air in a half-chuckle and said to himself (or possibly to the horses), "Dangerous plant, indeed."

He opened the top of the bag and peered inside. He had to admit, it was of a particular variety that he hadn't seen before, but around these parts, there couldn't be anything so strange, exotic and poisonous growing.

He pulled the bag off the harness and plunged his hand inside. He pulled a sprig of the stuff out and took a closer look, even smelt it. It had no smell, but it did look unusual, he thought.

"Those rebels were just telling a tale to get out of trouble," he said, throwing the stuff back in the bag and then hanging it back on the horse. "Come on," he said taking them both by the reins, "let's get you to the palace. Would you like to be a couple of Roman horses?" One of them puffed air through it's nostrils in protest.

Silius laughed lightheartedly, "Alright, have it your way. We'll just look after you until we can find you both a home, eh?"

He walked them in the direction of the king's palace, just as he started to feel an itch on the edge of his bottom lip.

"Hello!!" the Captain shouted again, when he thought he'd come closer to the sound. "Hello, hello!" This time, Paulo could've sworn the Captain called it out melodiously.

"There's no one around, we've been walking for ages!" said Paulo.

"Hey, there's nothing you can see that isn't shown."

". . . Huh?"

". . . I don't really know what that means. Basically, in other words, we haven't looked everywhere yet, so how do you know there's nobody around?

"But we can't look *everywhere*, we don't even know where we've been, there's no landmarks of any kind."

The Captain had stopped in his tracks by the time Paulo had finished what he was saying, and he was looking straight down at the ground with a grim look on his face.

"I would say this is a pretty distinct landmark."

Paulo caught up with the Captain and realised with a shock what he had meant. He swallowed and said worriedly, "Is he . . . is he dead?"

The Captain knelt down beside the motionless body lying on his stomach on the dusty desert ground. He put two fingers up to the poor man's neck to find a pulse, but there wasn't one. He stood up again. "I'd say for at least a couple of hours."

"Captain," Paulo then said as he spotted something else on the ground a little way ahead.

The Captain followed his eye line and jogged over to it. It was another poor soul in the same state as the first.

"What do you think they died of? Hunger? Thirst? Heat stroke?"

The Captain shook his head. "Don't know. I suppose it could have been any of tho . . . wait a minute."

"What?"

"What do you notice about both of them?"

"What do they have in common, you mean?"

"Mmm."

"Apart from the obvious?"

"Apart from the obvious," the Captain nodded quickly.

"Erm . . . they . . . both . . . um . . . I don't know. I give up."

"They're both facing the same way."

"Facing the same way?" Paulo looked at them both from where they were standing. "You're right. Both their heads are pointing in that direction."

"As if they were both heading the same way before they collapsed."

"Well what is it over there that they were so desperate to get to?" He pointed in the direction of where he and the Captain had come from.

"*Or*," said the Captain darkly, "what was it in *that* direction," he pointed the opposite way, "that they were trying to get away from?"

They both looked in *that* direction. Paulo felt a shiver run down his spine, even though it had to be at least fifty degrees Celsius out there. They started walking onward.

When Marius had returned to the house, he'd acted as if nothing had happened. He just grunted at Evie, ordering her to get back to her duties and then returned to the others and their cheerful conversation. But every time Evie passed the doorway to the outside courtyard, she always noticed that Marius was not ever completely absorbed in the discussion. He had a perpetual frown on his face and it was clear that the nods he was giving were just to make it appear as though he knew what the others were talking about.

In fact, it was the same for the rest of the morning and into the afternoon. Marius seemed always to be in a state of deep thought. Evie made sure she stayed well clear of him. He appeared never to be in a good mood and when the four of them ate together and chatted with each other, he always seemed preoccupied.

At mid-afternoon, Evie was called out into the courtyard where the four friends were lounging. She presented herself promptly and as soon as she appeared, she could feel Marius' eyes on her. When she looked at him, his stare seemed to pierce right through her and she felt instantly small and vulnerable. She could not look at him for very long. She suddenly thought that if she was older and braver, she could have kept staring him down, giving him a discreet look that said "I know you don't belong here, I know you've stolen the Train. And whatever it is you're up to, I'm going to find out what it is and put a stop to it."

But, alas, those eyes were too scary to look into, even for one second.

Marius spoke: "Let me look at her, yes . . . yes, she looks strong enough. Strong-willed if nothing else. And *young*. That is what I want, a *young* servant. Someone who will be able to serve me for years to come. Not someone I will have to throw on the scrap heap after a year or two."

Then Lucius spoke: "I don't understand, Marius. You're telling me you want to buy the girl from me?"

Evie's eyes widened. *Is this legal?* she thought.

"Yes. For a price of course."

"Of course."

Evie panicked. *I can't be bought! I'm a person!*

"But Lucius, we've only just acquired her," said Camilla. "I like her and I want to keep her."

Evie gave a subtle little nod to herself, feeling glad of Camilla's opinion.

"Well I like her too, but we haven't heard what Marius is prepared to pay. Living where we live in the king's grounds, we will find it easy to get another slave."

Evie had Lucius on one side of her and Marius on the other. In her mind, she was barracking for Camilla, willing her on to stick up for her some more.

"Evie is inexperienced," Camilla said, "you wouldn't want to have her as your slave. She is still learning."

Yay! Go Camilla! She used my name as well.

"I don't care. She's in good enough shape for me," said Marius. "Any other second hand slave will already have stripes on his back* and worn out joints."

"Well what if I said she is not for sale!" said Camilla.

---

* from being beaten and whipped by their masters.

Evie nodded and smiled energetically.

Lucius put a hand out to his wife to shush her, calm her down.

"What price would you offer?" Lucius asked.

Evie frowned again and looked across at Marius, waiting for his answer.

He eventually said, "Twenty shekels."

Evie's eyebrows rose. She had no concept of how much twenty shekels was, but to hear herself, her life, her whole identity being put down to a price—it felt weird and appalling. Plus, the Captain had paid twenty shekels for those robes in the market. She was worth more than that!

"Marius," said Portia, his wife, "We don't need another slave, what's the meaning of this?"

As if ignoring her, Marius said to Lucius, "What do you say to that?"

"No sale. I think the girl is worth more than that."

Evie gave a satisfied nod.

"Fifty shekels," said Lucius.

She frowned. Darn it, it wasn't over.

"Thirty," said Marius.

"Fifty. I will settle for no less."

Evie smiled again. *Yeah, you stay strong to your word Lucius!*

Marius sat back in his chair, stroking his beard. Then he looked at Lucius straight in the eyes. "I will give you forty shekels and my other slave Levi for her."

Evie's jaw uncontrollably dropped and she was frowning again. She gave a hopeful glance at Lucius. *Come on, say no. Say no—no sale! I don't want to stay here with Marius.*

But Lucius was thinking about it.

Portia said, "Marius no. What are you saying? I don't want to give Levi away. He's a good worker."

"He'll be a good worker for our friends."

"But Marius," said Lucius, "we seem to be getting the better deal here. You would exchange your young male slave for someone as weak and inexperienced as this girl?"

Marius would not take his eyes off Lucius. He maintained a burning, intimidating, relentless stare. "Whatever it takes."

Portia was clearly furious with her husband. But she remained silent from now on.

Evelyn was looking at Lucius as well, with a heavy breath and a pounding heart. *Don't say yes. Don't say yes. Please don't say yes . . .*

He shrugged slowly. "Alright, but I don't understand you."

Evie's shoulders sagged, and her mouth hung open again. She couldn't believe it. Neither could the wives evidently.

"We will shake on it. Let me have your mark of agreement."

Lucius leant forward and took Marius' hand. The shake was more or less right in front of Evie's face, and although she'd just been bought for a price, she suddenly felt worthless. She was a business transaction. A piece of merchandise. An item to be taken off a shelf and purchased. *How could they? How could Lucius do that? Why didn't you say something, Camilla? How could this happen to me?*

Chapter Thirteen

Coming Clean

The next thing Evie knew, there was talk of Lucius and Camilla leaving. She thought she must have heard wrong, for they had not planned to return home for another week yet. Their visit had only really just begun. *No, I must have misunderstood,* she thought.

Levi then came up behind her as she was hanging up some wet rags to dry. "Lucius and Camilla are leaving for home this evening."

"What? Why?"

"Do not ask of me, I have no answers," he said.

"I guess you'll be . . . packing up your things to go with them."

"Things?"

"Your belongings, you know. Things you own."

"I do not have any belongings. What do you think I am, a Roman? A free spirit?"

Evie could hear her inner-voice say *whoops.* Then she said, "Will you be sad to leave your home?"

"Not my home. It is Marius' home. It is Maruis' life I've lived."

"You know what I mean. You've been here for so long, it's like a home. You'll have to get used to a whole new place and routine and everything."

"I suppose so," he said, relaxing a little. "But I'm hoping it will be a nice change. Surely any master could not be as harsh as Marius."

"Harsh?" Evie said, feeling herself starting to tremble.

"I do not wish to frighten you, but I am glad it is you who are staying and I who is leaving."

"Marius really mean, huh?"

"Doesn't care for anybody except himself. Sometimes I don't even think he cares for his own wife. And if it is that way for the mistress, what treatment for the slave?" Levi left it as a rhetorical question, and passed Evie by.

Nice way of showing that you don't wish to frighten me, Evie thought. But then, her shakes disappeared when she remembered that there was something more about Marius than met the eye. He had a giant machine down in the basement that shouldn't be around yet for another few thousand years, and he was keeping it a secret even from his wife. Was he even from this time himself? Evie would never have dreamt of a solution like someone being in the wrong time. But now that she knew time travel was possible and indeed real, she thought that this was a very plausible possibility. She thought of the coin that had *plinked* out of Callista's pocket back at the other house, and thought maybe it was a good thing that she was staying here. Perhaps she could get to the bottom of it all.

Shortly afterwards, Camilla came and found Evelyn and pulled her aside for a quick chat before they had to rush off.

"Evelyn, I'm sorry about this," she said warmly.

"You don't have to say sorry. I'm only a slave. I do what I'm told, I go where I'm sent."

"I didn't want to sell you to my sister's husband, but he was so persistent, that brute of a man. And Lucius is always interested in a profit when he can find one."

"Why are you leaving so soon?"

"Lucius said he had things to do back home and the weather apparently is turning bad in a week and so travelling will be dangerous."

"Who told you that?"

"Marius. He was the one who brought these things to my husband's attention."

"But how can he tell what the weather's gonna be like in a week?" Evie didn't know much about ancient bible times, but she did at least know that they had no weather forecasting instruments. And certainly no T.V. weather channel to check the predictions.

"I do not know. Marius is an influential and very intelligent man, I find it difficult to contradict him."

"What if he's just making it up?"

"Why would he? Why would he want us to leave earlier than we had planned?"

"Because . . ." Evie almost burst out with a possible reason. That Marius didn't trust Evie and wanted to have her constantly under his surveillance and get rid of everyone else so as to keep his secret safe. But she didn't want to draw attention to herself. She was just a visitor in this world. And anything good or helpful she'd tried to do so far had only gotten her into trouble. ". . . I don't know."

"Camilla," called a voice from the front of the house, "Are you ready to leave?"

"Yes!" she called back. Then she looked at Evie with a warm, but pitiful smile, "You take care, Evelyn. Goodbye and good luck."

Evie gave her a grateful look. Surely this woman must have been the nicest woman to slaves in all of history.

Then Levi came past again. "I wish I could have gotten to know you a bit better," he said. "May God be your strength." He smiled and then disappeared.

She could hear their voices outside, saying farewell and then the horse starting to clop along the ground. She assumed everyone was out there, and that the house was empty, but she jumped in her skin when she realised Marius was standing at the other end of the room, leaning against the wall, staring at her.

He didn't move a muscle when she jumped. Just stood there with his arms folded.

After an excruciating moment of silence, Evie plucked up the courage and asked, "Why did you pay so much to have me as your slave?"

He had a creepy almost-smile on his face, and he said softly, "I don't trust you."

"I thought so." Choosing to keep out of trouble, Evie just said, "Well is . . . is there anything you want me to do . . . at the moment?"

"Come into the sitting room with a bowl of hot water, cloths and some soap," he said and then walked away.

Portia came back inside saying, "What a pity they had to leave so soon."

"Yes," said Marius. "It was in Lucius' best interest though."

"But surely Lucius had all his work under control since they'd planned to come here. And I just can't believe the change of weather that you think is going to happen. How do you know these things?"

"Because, my dear, I know everything," he said with a smile.

Coming into the room where he was sitting, Portia said, "That's no explanation." She came and sat down next to him on the floor cushions.* "And because of you and your unfathomable ways, I have to get used to an entirely new slave. Now why did you go and do that?"

"Well . . . I thought wives were supposed to submit to their husbands."

"I'm only asking for a reason. Surely you have one, don't you?"

"That's my business, woman."

Suddenly, Portia's mood went from a lighthearted nature, to an irritated and defensive one.

"Marius, I am your wife, not another of your slaves."

"Don't you need to go to the market?"

"I've already done that, early this morning."

"Well go and tend to the garden then, before the day is out. You're behind with all your duties because of our guests being here."

Portia felt infuriated inside, but she chose to contain it and obey her husband. She knew better than to argue with him too much. She went out to the garden, leaving Marius alone in the house. With Evie.

Evie, the slave, came into the sitting room with what Marius had asked for. She watched him take off his sandals and then he said, "Now you will wash my feet."

---

* Tall tables and chairs were not yet popular in these times and in this culture.

Uncontrollably, Evie's nose crinkled up as she looked down at his sweaty, dirty feet—hairy toes and all. An unintended "ughh," came out from her mouth.

Marius' face went red with anger. "You are lucky your back is not slashed with stripes for sneaking down into that cellar. You are my slave now. And you'll do as I say."

Hanging up on the wall in one of the other rooms, she remembered seeing a whip. Thick, leather bands draping from the handle. She could just about feel the lashes, imagine the constant stinging on her back. It was either that, or wash this dude's feet.

She knelt down opposite him with the bowl and the cloths and started the job. It was the weirdest and creepiest thing that she'd ever done in her life and it was the most awkward silence that could ever exist. It became even worse when he started talking to her.

"You're not from here are you?"

She shook her head.

"Where are you from?"

"Bethlehem," she said.

He made one quick exhale of air—a chuckle, like he immediately didn't believe her.

She glanced up at him with just her eyes and then quickly back down again to what she was doing.

He folded his arms. "Where did you go to, to have your name marked on the census?"

Evie didn't understand what he was talking about. And it showed. She thought quickly for an answer. "Where I was meant to go."

He leaned closer to her, his face so frightening. "Where did you go for the census?"

". . . Where everyone goes for the census."

He gave a little grunt and leant back against the cushions behind him.

She thought she had outsmarted him, but he kept coming at her with the questions.

"Where were you born? You don't look Judean."

Evie hated lying. She hated that prickly feeling she got all over her face when she was making up a story and passing it off as the truth. Every time, she could feel her face flaring up like a red flag waving the words LIAR, but hoped hopelessly the receiver of the lie wouldn't notice. Besides, she always felt so guilty afterwards and paranoid about the truth coming out. So she tried to get away with telling as much truth as possible.

"I wasn't born in Bethlehem."

"So where?"

"Far away." *How silly,* she thought, *that sounded so deliberately secretive.*

"What *town?*" he demanded.

"It's a small little place called . . . Adelaide." She said it so quietly and quickly, she hoped he'd be satisfied.

"Where?" He narrowed his eyes.

"It's so small, you wouldn't have heard of it."

"And you haven't always been a slave?"

"No. In fact right up until two days ago I wasn't a slave."

"Yes, Portia's sister said something about that."

Marius seemed to be in his own little world of thought as she was answering his questions. Evie decided to pull him out of it. In order for her to relax in a social situation, she always resorted to asking her own questions. Maybe it would work here as well.

So . . . here we go. ". . . Where are *you* from?" she asked Marius.

It clearly surprised him, because his whole body language changed from aggressive to defensive.

"That is none of your business, slave-girl." He made sure to add on her new name at the end.

"But I don't think of myself as a slave. And I've seen quite a few Roman people now, and to me, you don't look Roman."

"You're talking nonsense."

"It's something in your eyes. No . . . it's your nose. I don't know, there's something about your face that's not right."

"Silence. You will speak when you are spoken to, slave-girl."

And there was silence for a short time. Until Evie said, "So . . . ? Where *are* you from?"

"You're not afraid of me much are you?"

Evie was very much afraid of him. But she was trying not to show it. Apparently, she was doing a good job.

She saw no harm in lying about this one. "Nup," she said. She was dying to talk more about the machine downstairs. But there was no chance he'd cooperate and tell her about that. She also remembered his words last night:

You will not speak of or think any more of this. If you do, I will get rid of you.

She had no idea what this man was capable of, and she didn't fancy flirting with the possibility of the whole thing being a bluff.

Perhaps if she had some leverage. Something that might frighten him a bit. Now, he was not the sort of creature you'd imagine being frightened of *anything*, but there had to be something. She remembered that in movies, to scare some crook, the police would tell the victim to use the word 'we' a lot. Make them feel like they're outnumbered. Evelyn was just the tip of the ice-berg, and underneath the water's surface there was an army waiting to come and help. Surely Paulo and the Captain were out there looking for her. They would have to make do as the army.

"I'll tell you the truth," Evie suddenly heard herself saying.

Marius waited, with an attentive ear.

"We're very interested in what you have downstairs and I'm, we're going to find it difficult to forget about it."

Marius looked unconvinced. "Who is 'we'?"

"I have some friends who are on their way to find me and they're going to agree with me when I say that King Herod should be informed."

"Who are your friends," he said skeptically.

"A team led by who I believe is the most intelligent and skilful man on this planet."

"You're playing games with me, girl. And *that* is a very big mistake. You will live to regret it if you try and cross me. In fact, you may not even live at all. Do you comprehend?"

Evie tried not to look scared. She tried to arrange her facial features into a confident smile—as if there was some big joke being withheld from him.

But Marius did not look phased at all. His face looked calmer and smugger than ever. But then suddenly, he stood up in one sharp motion, causing the bowl of soapy water to tip over, and water splashed everywhere. Evie jumped backwards onto her feet and kept backing away, as he kept on moving towards her.

"You are playing with fire, girl. Do you realise that?" he growled at her. "You don't believe I will stay true to my word. But I can and I will."

"Y-you'll go to jail for that, won't you?"

"Ha!!" He then walked past her, which Evie wasn't expecting. But then, when she realised where he was heading, a chill ran down her spine and a terrible sinking feeling in her stomach made her feel sick. He reached his hand up onto that wall and took down the whip. When he came back into the room, Evie was backing away as far as she could get from him, without taking her eyes off him. But soon she realised all she had done was back herself into a corner—from which there was no escape.

He was advancing on her, step by step. It was just like a nightmare. She called out for help, but nobody could hear her. Portia was well away from the house and the houses in this small town were far away from one another.

"No, please!" she shouted.

"Tell me everything then," he growled. "Or soon you will wish I'd killed you before."

"No! I can't! I-I'm nobody, really!"

He reached out one of his giant hands and grabbed her violently by the arm. He yanked her body around so that her back was facing him. Evie knew he was about to whip her as a way to get her to talk, but she couldn't let this happen. She made one last effort to get away. She sprung off of her right foot, lurching to the left. Then three things happened all in one split second. First, she broke free of his grasp, but then she felt him catch her again on her way out of the corner. But something had happened, which made him let go and his face showed some kind of shock.

What had happened? Why was he looking at her this way? When Evie was almost through the doorway nearby, she realised suddenly, that in his hand, Marius was holding her torn robe. Her rolled up jeans, pink T-shirt and favourite hooded-jacket were all revealed. She looked down at her clothes and then back up to Marius' face.

His reaction was most interesting. It wasn't Lucius' confused bewilderment, as though he was looking at something he'd never seen before. It was a wide-eyed, astonished realisation. But even though Marius appeared surprised and caught off-guard, somehow, he was even more frightening than before.

Chapter Fourteen

The Purple Predator

There had been more bodies along the way. The Captain and Paulo kept following them across the dry desert landscape. They were all heading in different directions, but they were all heading *away* from the same direction. That much was clear. But there was something important that wasn't clear.

"What did they all die from, Captain?" asked Paulo.

"I'm not one hundred percent sure, but one thing is certain."

"What's that?"

"They all died the same way."

"Must have been the environment. There's nothing out here to eat or drink, no shelter, nothing."

"I think it's the environment alright, but I don't think it was lack of food, drink or shelter."

"Why not?"

"Look," the Captain said kneeling over one of the bodies. "This man isn't skinny, his skin isn't dehydrated or even sun burnt. Wherever we are, there isn't a lack of food, drink or shelter. I think if one was to walk around for a bit, one would find sufficient provisions for one's survival. In fact, look, just over there, there's a pool of water and some trees."

"Could be a mirage."

"Well let's see."

They walked about fifty metres and arrived at a real pool of real water and three real trees with real fruit growing on them. The Captain knelt down by the water, cupped his hands, dipped them in the water and tasted it.

"Is it any good?"

"Fine," said the Captain.

"Good, I'm parched!" Paulo took a drink, while the Captain tried the fruit. It was edible and very tasty.

Once they had finished the quite-satisfying meal, the Captain said, "This only proves my point. If this is here, there would be other trees and pools of water around the place. There's no way all these people died of thirst, hunger or anything else quite as natural as that." He walked back over to one of the bodies and tried to examine it more closely.

"He's still a little warm," said the Captain. "If my theory is correct, we must be getting close to whatever killed them.

"There is something else I've noticed.

"What's that Paulo?"

"Well the first lot of people we came across seemed to be, sort of healthier looking or something, and in their prime, you know sixteen, seventeen or eighteen."

"You mean in their twenties or thirties?" ♣

"Yes, sorry, I keep forgetting."

♣ Remembering that on Serothia, someone who was thirty-two like Paulo, was only seventeen in Earth years.

"You're right though, Paulo. All of these where we are now seem either old and frail or just less well built."

"I even saw a young four year old."

"You mean a young fifteen year old."

"Yes. But what does it mean?"

"I think I know," he said with a look of dread on his face. "But I also think if we kept walking a little way, we'll know for sure. If I'm right, those who have stronger, healthier bodies lived longer and covered more ground before they died, where as these . . ."

"Weren't as strong and so were among the first to die?"

"Correct. Let's keep walking."

Paulo grabbed the Captain's arm. "But is it safe? We might end up joining all these people spread all over the land."

"If I'm right, we can choose not to."

"But what if you're not right?"

"I'm ninety-nine percent sure that I'm right, come on."

"But what about that one percent? There's still a chance you're wrong."

"Oh come on! Stop being such a worry wart." He said it kindly, but it made Paulo gulp down a big lump in his throat before carrying on, walking right behind the Captain.

Suddenly, the Captain stopped. "Oh, now I'm one hundred percent sure."

"What? Why?"

They had come to a man lying on the ground. He had evidently died on his back, with his face staring up to the sky.

Paulo gasped when he saw the face. "What's that terrible rash?" Paulo knelt down to take a closer look. "It's all purple and blotchy and . . ."

"Don't touch it," the Captain said and then looked up at the way ahead of them.

"Do you think they've all been like this and we just couldn't see it?"

"I have no doubt. But I wish I was wrong." He spoke slowly and solemnly. "Come on, Paulo. We might be able to stop this from happening again." This time, the Captain started running, and Paulo found it nearly impossible to keep up with him.

"Captain!" he called after him. "What is it? What's so . . ."

He caught up. The Captain had stopped again. He was standing at the very edge of a sea of luscious purplely-green undergrowth.

When Paulo could find his voice, he muttered in disbelief, looking out onto the expanse of deadly ground. "Kratilier Lumis." And after a moment of silence, he looked up at the Captain and said, "As you suspected?"

The Captain nodded.

"We can't dig all this up."

The Captain shook his head. "The only solution is if we burn it all, in the ground."

"But the fumes, surely . . ."

He shook his head again. "Fumes are harmless. It'll be fine, we just need to find a match, that's all. There's no rain out here, it'll be as dry as anything. Should catch quite nicely."

Marius had been staring at Evie for a good ten seconds. For every one of those seconds, she was devising the best route of escape.

"What are you doing in those clothes?" Marius asked in a quiet voice, holding back his great strength and anger.

1, 2, 3 . . . Go. Evie made a run for it. Through the front room and out the door. But once she was outside, she had no idea where to run. It was that split second hesitation that let her down. Marius grabbed hold of her arms again and she struggled and struggled to pull free. But she was wasting all of her energy. Marius was far too strong for her.

"Who are you?" Marius demanded of her in a terrifyingly calm voice. She looked up fearfully into his eyes. She pondered for a second who it was between them that was in control. He needed to know who she was and whether she posed a threat to him and his mysterious machine. And so she figured that for as long as she kept this information from him, he would keep her alive.

"Come on, speak up!"

"My name is Evie Bamford," she answered truthfully.

"And . . . ?"

"And seeing as my secretiveness is what's keeping me alive, that's all I'm telling you."

His upper lip quivered in annoyance.

Just then, Portia called from a distance away in the garden. "Marius! There are some people here to see you."

Evie and Marius looked at each other. Evie hoped and prayed it was the Captain and Paulo, and Marius didn't want to take any chances. He hauled her back into the house and dragged her towards the closed door, which led to the downstairs room. He opened the door and tossed her inside causing her to tumble a little way down the steps. Then he came into the darkness after her and carried her all the way down to the bottom and into the underground room. He threw her down onto the floor against the wall, then quickly grabbed some rope, tied her wrists up in it and then tied the rope to a hook on the wall above her head, where the torch or lantern was usually hung.

All the way down, Evie had been pushing and shoving to try and break free. She'd called out, "Help! Let me go!" to which he'd simply said, "Shut up!" and continued his task.

He now said to her, his face so close to hers, his breath made her eyes blink, "No one will ever find you. And whatever it is you're hiding, be sure that I will find out what it is. And it is up to you whether I find out the easy way or the hard way."

He stood up, turned and started walking back up the steps, leaving the place in total darkness.

But before disappearing out of sight completely, he turned his face back to her and said with an evil smile, "Don't go anywhere will you?"

"And how do you suppose we find a match out here," said Paulo, looking around him.

"I don't. Especially seeing as they haven't been invented yet."

"Well I learnt how to start a fire with stones when I was a kid," said Paulo.

"So did I. But have you seen a flint stone anywhere around."

Paulo shook his head, hopelessly. "Well haven't you got a gadget in one of your pockets that could do the trick? I mean, you've got things like your Atom Relocating Molecular Teleport Device, your Portable Audio Clandestine Digital Communicator . . ."

"I know," he clicked his finger. "Of course, I forgot, I have my Manual Hand Operating Fuel Injected Flame Combustion Apparatus. Paulo, you're a genius."

"What's that?"

The Captain took out of his pocket a tiny, rectangular object. "A cigarette lighter."

"Don't tell me you smoke."

"Paulo, people use lighters for lots of things, not just cigarettes."

"Like burning the Violet Assassin for instance," Paulo smiled.

"Exactly. Besides, do you think someone as clever as me would do something so silly?"

"I guess not."

Then the Captain lit the Manual Hand Operating Fuel Injected Flame Combustion Apparatus. "Right," he said and knelt down, holding the flame by the very first leaf of the Violet Assassin.

"Careful, Captain," said Paulo, noticing that the Captain's finger was getting quite close to the leaf in order for the flame to touch it.

"Come on, come on," muttered the Captain, "Catch light. Catch light."

It caught, and there was a tiny flame burning away at that one leaf of the purple plant. They watched in anticipation, the Captain starting to smile as the flame grew bigger.

But soon, his smile dropped as the flame dwindled suddenly, and in the next second, it was gone, leaving only a little swirl of smoke rising up and disappearing into the air.

Paulo frowned. "That's not supposed to happen is it?"

"Definitely not. I'd better try again." The Captain knelt down again and repeated steps one to three, then stood up and watched again . . . as the flame did the same thing as before.

"It should've caught light," mumbled the Captain.

"I gathered that. What's wrong?"

"Perhaps it needs kindling to get it started. Perhaps it is slighlty wet."

"What a shame we can't touch it to find out. Wait, the rest of the ground's as dry as anything, the plant can't be wet."

"I'll try once more." He knelt down, lit another leaf, tried lighting a few, but they all dwindled down and the Violet Assassin was left more or less unharmed.

"Well," said the Captain, standing up and putting the lighter back in his pocket. "You learn something new everyday. Kratilier Lumis does not burn."

"Well that's just wonderful."

"Now, now. Please, no sarcasm." He scratched his head.

"What if there was a huge fire—already started, would it burn then, do you think."

"I honestly don't know."

"Well there must be some way to control it. Otherwise, that jungle where you said it grows must be just covered in the stuff. It would spread and spread and spread!"

"That's it!" said the Captain, grabbing Paulo around the shoulders. "You're a double genius! The jungle!"

"You mean the home of the Violet Assassin? What about it?"

"The fact is, the jungle where this stuff is found is *not* covered in it. In fact, I happen to know that it's kept very well under control. There's some natural process that goes on in that jungle environment that keeps it under control. All I have to do is figure out what that natural process is."

"But how? Go to the jungle?"

"In a sense. I'll look it up."

"Look it up? How?"

"On my databank. All we need to do is find the Train!"

Paulo's shoulders sank and he sighed, closing his eyes. "So we're back where we started. Finding the Train."

He looked at Paulo, nodded and said frankly, "Yes."

CAPTAIN!!

"Did you hear that?" said the Captain.

Paulo shook his head.

"I thought I heard someone calling . . ."

"CAPTAIN!!"

Paulo whipped his head around, "I heard it that time. Someone's calling you!"

"Hello?" called the Captain.

"Captain!!!" cried the voice.

The two were scanning the landscape carefully, and suddenly Paulo spotted a horse in the distance, galloping towards them. "Captain! Over there!" he said, pointing.

The Captain started running over to the horse and soon saw that there was a Roman soldier riding it, and he was the one calling out.

"Captain!! Please! Help me!"

When the Captain and the horse came nearer to each other, the Roman said, "Thank the gods," and then collapsed, sliding off the horse and falling onto the ground in a heap.

The Captain ran over to him and rolled him onto his back. "It's Silius!" he said to Paulo in alarm.

Silius appeared to be choking on something, but as soon as the Captain noticed a small spread of purple rash in the corner of his mouth, he knew exactly what was wrong.

He had trouble speaking, but he managed to say, "I didn't believe you about the plant, Captain. But now I must apologise . . ."

"Shhh," said the Captain, "It's alright. What you need now is an antidote."

"Is there one?" said Paulo.

"I touched the plant you had in the bag," Silius continued, "and I must have . . ."

"Shhh, never mind that, now. Since something foreign has entered your system, something non-foreign might fix it up. I don't know for sure, but it's worth a try, only we must work fast."

"What is there we can use?" Paulo asked.

"Well, he has to actually consume it . . . I know! The fruit tree! Paulo, run over and pick one of those fruits! Quickly!"

Paulo obeyed while the Captain tried to keep Silius conscious. He seemed to want to lay his head down and go to sleep but the Captain knew that if he fell asleep, he may never wake up again. "Silius, I know you want to rest, but you can't, you have to stay with me! Erm . . . what's the day of the week?"

"I don't know," he said breathlessly. "My mind's gone blank, my head feels all fuzzy."

"Okay, tell me what it feels like. Your throat, tell me exactly what it feels like in your throat?"

"Like there is fungus growing . . . inside my mouth and around my lips. Itchy. Very itchy. Crawling."

"Paulo! Hurry up with that fruit!!"

"Will I live, Captain?"

"Yes! You'll be fine, just stay awake!" What he really meant was, *I honestly don't know, but this is the only thing I can try!*

"Here," said Paulo rushing to the Captain.

"Right Silius, eat this."

"No, I can't. Can't feel my mouth anymore."

"You have to. The plant is attacking your nervous system! That means you must eat the fruit now, or you'll die!"

Silius grabbed the Captain's hand with the fruit in it and took as big-a-bite as he could manage.

"Please let this work," mumbled the Captain. "Please let this work."

"What should it do?" asked Paulo.

"The natural particles inside this native fruit could work as antibodies to fight the foreign material in his system. Besides, give him some extra vitamins at the same time."

"Fingers crossed," said Paulo.

"What good's that going to do? Don't tell me you have superstition on Serothia as well?"

"It's very popular."

"Put your trust in something real, for goodness sake."

Silius kept on taking more and more bites of the fruit, and with each bite, he seemed to be getting stronger.

"How do you feel?"

"My throat feels clearer, I think."

The Captain smiled, "Keep eating!"

"This is delicious," said Silius. "I haven't eaten one of these since I was a boy, I think."

"That's great, how do you feel now?"

"Well I can feel every part of my mouth again . . . It's Tuesday."

The Captain let out a huge joyful laugh, looking up to the heavens. "It worked! It worked!"

"Praise the gods," said Silius, still a little weak.

"There's only one God you need to thank, Silius. Here, finish your fruit. Can you stand up?"

"Yes, I think so." As he stumbled up onto his feet, Paulo noticed that the purple on his face had diminished a little.

"Hey, even the rash is disappearing," Paulo said. "Well that's handy to know. We'll carry some of this fruit along with us, shall we?"

"Good idea," said the Captain. Then he looked at the horse that had carried the soldier here. "Hey, I recognise you!" He patted him on the nose. "You're one of Elisha's faithful horses. Good to see you again."

"The other one," Silius said, a little breathlessly and dusting himself off, "is still outside the palace." Then he said to the Captain, "A thousand pardons again, Captain whoever you are. I now realise how dangerous that plant was."

"Well there's a lot more around the place that still needs to be dealt with."

"Where has it come from?"

"Somewhere else," said Paulo, using the Captain's words.

"You mean, another city?"

"Well, a little further than that."

Silius looked confused. "Well what can be done about it? If it's not controlled soon, it will be like a plague."

"I need to find something. Something that belongs to me. And then I'll be able to start coming up with a plan."

"Tell me what it is, and I will help you. I'll lead you straight back to Jerusalem if that is where you need to go."

The Captain breathed in and out deeply and then pulled out a gadget from one of his pockets. This time, it was a tiny circular shaped thing. Smaller than the lighter.

"What is it this time," Paulo asked, looking at the little metal disk.

"Nothing," he said. "Absolutely nothing. I should have been getting signals from this thing. I hope it's not broken." He gave it a shake.

"What is it?"

"It's a Unique Radio-Wave-Operated Link Chip. I own two. One of them is here in my hand and the other one is inside the Train. They can talk to each other in a sense, allowing me to locate the Train if I ever forget where I parked it. Very handy in shopping centre car parks."

Paulo was astonished. "Then why, for goodness sake, didn't you bring it out earlier?"

"I did. I just didn't tell you about it, because I was hoping to spare you from the bad news."

"Bad news?"

"There was no signal when we were back in Bethlehem. And there's still no signal now."

"Oh no. The one in the Train must have conked out."

"Impossible. No, I think the only explanation, is that the Train simply does not exist. Not currently, anyway. It has been taken completely out of time and space."

Chapter Fifteen

All Freed Up And Nowhere To Go

Stuck, Evelyn thought. *What good am I to anyone now?* She complained to herself. *I had to go and open my big mouth, didn't I. I should have known that speaking up and trying to do some private investigating would only get me into more trouble.* Then different thoughts came to her. *I suppose this is better than slaving away upstairs. I should be thankful I didn't get a whipping. I should be thankful I'm still alive.*

Well, she said to herself, *this is what I wanted I guess. To be in this room again with this machine. Except I can't do anything about it because one: I can't see it; and two: I can't reach it.*

She sighed out loud.

Then she thought she'd have one more go, see if she could get her voice even louder than she did three minutes ago.

"HELP!!!!"

Her voice bounced off the four stone walls and was absorbed up into the earth surrounding them. This was a mighty deep hole in the ground, she doubted whether even the 'H' reached as far as half way up the flight of steps.

She sighed again, and then thought about praying. "Well, it's worked before," she said to herself. "Dear Lord, thank you that so far, you've kept me safe and unharmed. I pray that you protect Paulo and the Captain as well, and most of all, I pray that they'll find me down here and rescue me. I pray that we can get the Train back . . ." then she stopped, staring into the blackness in front of her—about where the mysterious, futuristic machine sat. She decided that it couldn't be too far away from her—it was only a small room. She might be able to reach it with her feet if she stretched her body out as far as it could stretch. Maybe then, she might be able to switch it on and attract the attention of Mr Scary and whoever his visitors were! After all, it made that humming noise that she couldn't ignore last night, and the buzzing sound it made when turned on *was* pretty loud. She shuffled her bottom away from the wall—as far as it could go without it actually lifting off the ground. Then she stretched out her legs until every muscle in them was aching and it almost felt like they could slip out of their sockets. She flayed them around on the floor in the hope that she'd hit gold—namely: part of the machine.

She was bashing the lower half of her body around fiercely and finally, when she reached her right leg out just that little bit more, her foot caught on part of the machine.

"There it is," she said, but then her spirit sank again. "Now what? Your foot can touch the very edge of the machine. Big deal." But after a few seconds of hard thinking, she realised the ropes around her wrists felt looser than before—after all that wriggling around. "Maybe I don't need hard thinking, maybe all I need is a little positive thinking."

She twisted her wrists to and fro between the ropes, trying to expand and contract her muscles so as to loosen the ropes more. It was working a little bit, but the ropes still had a firm grip on her. She didn't give up for one moment though. If she'd loosened them a little way, she could loosen them more.

Evie's patience was tested. The time it took for her to wriggle free completely from the ropes was much longer than the time it has taken you to read this sentence. But eventually, yes, she did pull free, and she stood up immediately, giving her arm muscles a good stretch and rubbing her sore wrists. Now she could go straight to that light that turned the whole machine on. She knew exactly where it was, and she didn't hesitate to place her finger over it this time.

On it came with a click and that same low rumble as before. The loud buzzing started and then reduced to that low constant hum that sounded like the fan in the computer at home. She looked up in the direction of the stairs and unfortunately, there was no movement. She returned her attention back onto the machine and wondered whether she'd be able to get that image of the Train up again. Maybe she'll take *advantage* of the fact that nobody could hear her down here.

Now, what was it I pressed last time? It was one that I confused with the 'off/on' switch! So it must be near there!

She pressed a button next to the 'on' button. A few more lights came on, but nothing else. She pushed another one, (none of them had labels on them). Suddenly, an electronic voice said, "TUESDAY. SEVENTEENTH DAY. OCTOBER. THE YEAR, 4 B.C. EARTH TIME."

Although Evie was quite interested in knowing what the date was, she frowned. It was not the button she wanted.

She went to press another one nearby, a black one. But then thought twice. "No," she said to herself, "A button that's black probably means self destruct or something."

So instead, she went to the only other one which was near the 'on' switch—a big round red button.

The second she'd pressed it, all the lights on the machine started flashing a bright red colour and there was a loud, intrusive bleeping, screaming out from the machine's insides. Evie looked around with just her eyes, wondering what she'd done. Then the electronic voice started to relay out, "EMERGENCY SELF-DESTRUCTION PROCEDURE ACTIVATED. EMERGENCY SELF-DESTRUCTION PROCEDURE ACTIVATED. CLEAR AREA IMMEDIATELY. CLEAR AREA IMMEDIATELY. SAFETY GATE CLOSING. SAFETY GATE CLOSING. EMERGENCY SELF-DESTRUCTION IN 20, 19 . . ."

Evie didn't know what to do, but she then realised there was only one thing she could do. She just had to run back up the steps as quickly as she could and then get in big, life-threatening trouble with Marius. But another part of her wanted to scream at the machine, "No! You can't self-destruct! I've got to use you to get the Train back!!!"

"14, 13, 12 . . ."

I've got no choice! I've got to get out of here! She finally turned around and made a B-line for the steps, but instead of climbing up them, her body slammed into a flat metal wall. She staggered back. *What the . . . ?*

The short length of metal wall was a door standing between her and her way out. There was a crack down the middle as if the wall had slid shut from either side as soon as the self-destruct procedure had been activated. Evie suddenly realised with dread, "Safety gate!!"

"7, 6, 5, 4 . . ."

"Oh Lord!" she cried out. "Save me!"

"3, 2, 1 . . ."

For Evelyn, everything went black.

They were nearly out of the desert. Paulo and the Captain, absolutely exhausted; Silius draped over the saddle of the horse, still weak and recovering from a bad case of the Violet Assassin.

"Look, you can just see the outskirts of the city," said Silius.

"Good," said Paulo. "I'm tired of walking."

"But what do we do once we get there?" said the Captain, more so to himself.

"I thought you were the one who *answers* the questions, Captain."

"Well it's like longing for something like . . . success, or riches, or the next episode of *Lost In Space*. When you finally get there, you think—*now what?* You find it hasn't fulfilled you and satisfied you like you thought it would."

"Well it's a . . . start, isn't it?"

"I don't know. It could be a step backwards for all I know. That Violet Assassin in the desert isn't going to clear away by itself, perhaps I could have been of more use back there."

"I've never seen you so indecisive," said Paulo.

"That's because I'm hardly ever indecisive," the Captain replied. Then he reconsidered. "Or maybe it's because you haven't known me for very long. I can't decide which."

"Maybe we could somehow let the king know, this Herod guy, about the Violet Assassin and how it's killing people out here. The people he's banished."

"What would that do?" said Silius. "Herod is not bothered about what happens to those who have been banished. When he banishes them, it is as though he washes his hands of them."

"That's terrible!" said Paulo. "What kind of a king . . ."

"This is a very different world from what you're used to, Paulo," said the Captain. "There's much more evil here. There's cold blooded killing and there's deliberate deceit. There's lying and selfishness, hatred and rebellion. There are wars and evil rulers and people who think they're in control of the world and their own lives. Thank God there's now a Saviour on this earth—small as He is though at the moment.

"You mean the baby?" Paulo asked.

"What are you talking about, Saviour?"

"You'll see. In about thirty years or so. Now, where was I?"

"I was talking about telling Herod about the plant," said Paulo.

"That's right!"

"You think it will work?"

"No, no, that won't do any good. What we need is . . ."

"What?"

"What we need is . . ." he clicked his fingers repeatedly.

"Is *what?*"

"What did you say earlier?" he asked Silius.

"Um . . . I don't know, er . . . that we're nearly back at the city."

"No after that."

"Erm . . . that Herod isn't bothered with what . . ."

"A little bit after that."

"Well you started talking about some kind of saviour."

"No, before that."

There was a long pause. "About Herod . . . he washes his hands of those who are banished?"

"Yes," said the Captain, his finger doing its last, more decisive click. "You know Silius, you're not as Sillyous as you look."

"What do you mean?"

"Wash his hands. Like you were 'washed' in a sense of the Violet Assassin's attack. We'll *wash the Violet Assassin!*"

"Wash the Violet Assassin?" said Paulo, confused.

"Now now, Paulo, remember it was *my* idea."

"I don't get it."

"Well since I don't have my Train databank, we'll have to improvise. Now, this fruit cured Silius of the infection. It not only stopped further infection, it reversed the effects. What if, we make a big 'bath' of the stuff, you know, juiced it down and drenched the plant in it? What do you think?"

"Do you think that would work?" said Silius.

"No idea! But it's worth a try and I'm sorry Paulo, but it means more walking. First, we need a big container, or lots of little ones, and then we need to pick as much of this fruit as we can find."

Paulo couldn't help it, but he let out a little sigh, only thinking of how much work this was going to be.

"Come on! Where's your enthusiasm?" The Captain grabbed both Silius and Paulo around the shoulders and squeezed them. "Here's our chance to save the world again!"

Chapter Sixteen

The Return Of The Faithful Friend

Everything was still black. But the funny thing was, Evie could see the blackness. She was still alive! *How could this be?* Then the electronic voice sounded, "SELF-DESTRUCTION PROCEDURE FAILED. ENTITY STILL WITHIN VORTEX. SELF-DESTRUCTION PROCEDURE FAILED. ENTITY STILL WITHIN VORTEX. CANNOT PROCEED. PLEASE REMOVE ENTITY FROM VORTEX. CANNOT PROCEED. PLEASE REMOVE ENTITY FROM VORTEX."

What on earth does that mean? Evie thought to herself. *Whatever it is, it's good news for me.* Then, as if answering her question, light suddenly flooded the room. She turned around and . . .

Finally! There was the Train. An image of the Train anyway, floating above that same white light as before.

"There you are," said Evie, walking up to it. "Now I've just got to figure out how to get you out of the vortex apparently."

At that moment, she noticed a yellow light flashing on and off subtly, lighting up the words: RELEASE AND MATERIALISE.

The machine was telling her to release the entity from the vortex! *Clever thing.*

"This has got to work," she told herself.

She pressed the button underneath the words and a great big whoosh of sound filled her ears and more light illuminated the room—this time it was a concentration of blue light over to the left of the machine that for one second seemed to take the shape of the Train. Then it was gone and the only light in the room was provided by the small lights speckled all over the machine again.

I wonder, Evie thought and she walked quickly over to where the blue flash had been. She held her arms out in front of her,♣ feeling for the smooth metal surface of the side of the Train.

For a fraction of a second, she thought all her hopes were going to be dashed—there was nothing there. But one step further proved to be all she needed to feel that smooth paintwork, that wonderful, magical machine. A rescue ship out on a rough, stormy ocean. A familiar and faithful friend. A way out. The Train.

She wondered if she could get inside it. But when she found her way to the door, it was locked and she didn't have a key.

Then there was a sudden beeping coming from Marius' machine and the voice sounded again: "SELF-DESTRUCTION PROCEDURE INTERRUPTED. SELF-DESTRUCTION PROCEDURE INTERRUPT-ED. TURN OFF POWER TO ABORT; RESUMING SELF-DESTRUCTION IN 10, 9, 8 . . ."

♣   like people tend do when they're pretending to sleepwalk or look like a ghost. (Beats me too, I've never seen a ghost walk this way.)

Evie leapt over to the controls in a panic and her hands landed down hard on the 'on/off' button she now knew so well. "Abort I think!" she said.

The whole thing shut down. The lights, the humming and the buzzing all ceased in an instant. Evie breathed a sigh of utter relief. "That was close."

There was a mysterious beeping noise, but the Captain, Paulo and Silius were all searching hard for more of the rich, juicy, native fruit trees.

"We've got lots," said Paulo, running out of breath. "But we'll need millions to make enough juice to soak that field of Kratilier Lumis!"

"Kratoolia *Who*mis?" said Silius.

"The Violet Assassin."

"Oh."

Beep . . . beep . . . beep . . . beep . . .

"Could we dilute it?" asked Silius.

"Possibly," said the Captain. "But I don't want to rely on just a possibility. This problem is on such a big scale that I need our first attempt at fixing it to be the best one possible."

Beep . . . beep . . . beep . . . beep . . .

"I can see another tree over there!" said Paulo.

"Right, come along."

They all ran over. Silius was feeling much stronger by now and so he wasn't holding the others back at all. The horse was trotting along with them wherever they went so that they could stack him up with bags and bags of the fruit. *

---

* The bags were made out of anything they could find on the horse, like rugs and blankets. There were already two

"These look perfectly ripe," said Silius. "Just right for juicing, my aunt would say."

Beep . . . beep . . . beep . . . beep . . .

"Good," said the Captain. "I don't know what we're going to juice them in, but we'll cross that bridge when we come to it."

"We're running out of space to put them," said Paulo, while plucking fruits, two at a time from the tree.

"Well we'll cross that bridge when we come to it, too."

"We're crossing that bridge *now*, Captain."

Beep . . . beep . . . beep . . . beep . . .

"Okay, well we'll have to—what *is* that mysterious beeping noise?" he suddenly said irritably.

"It's coming from your pocket!" Paulo answered. He'd been wondering what it was for ages now, but he was waiting for the Captain to mention it.

"Is it? Oh!!" the Captain exclaimed, as if in sudden realisation. He dug deep down in his trouser pocket and whipped out the Unique Radio-Wave-Operated Link Chip. It was beeping like mad. He stared at it for a few seconds, gave it a shake, and then laughed out loud like a mad man.

"What? What is it?" asked Paulo.

"The Train! It exists! It's come back into space and time!"

"Does that mean someone's been flying the thing?" Paulo asked in sudden astonishment.

---

canvas bags and there was even a big basket on the back of the saddle, which Elisha already had on there when he lent it to Paulo and the Captain. They also had the Captain's robe.

"I don't know. I don't know how, what, when, where, who or why. All I know is, it's back in existence and I can track it now! Sorry, did I say I didn't know *where*? Of course I know where. All I have to do is follow this radio wave. It's in . . ." he held the gadget up like a compass and rotated his body around in a circle and then stopped. ". . . that direction."

"What about the fruit?" asked Paulo. "The Violet Assassin?"

"You two better keep picking them. We need as many as we can find."

"But how can we carry them all?" asked Silius.

"You're clever, Silius. I just know you'll be able to think of something. When you think you've got all you can get, meet me back at the palace. And if you come across Evelyn at any point . . . well, bring her along too."

"Of course," said Paulo. "You don't think I'm just going to leave her do you?"

"Good man." He patted Paulo on the back.

"Captain, why don't you use your teleporty thing now? I mean, you have to try and find the Train fast."

"Because I don't know the precise location until I arrive. Difficult to set coordinates. Besides, I don't believe the time is ripe. I have to choose carefully when I use my Atom Relocating Molecular Teleport Device. I just don't *feel* it yet."

"Twenty-four hours."

The Captain nodded. Then he shook both Silius and Paulo's hands. "Good luck."

"Good luck to you too, Captain," said Paulo.

And the Captain set off briskly in the direction he'd been shown by the Unique Radio-Wave-Operated Link Chip.

In the deep, musty gloom of this weird underground prison, Evelyn was in total silence again. The thick metal 'safety gate' had reopened when the machine's self-destruction procedure failed and she had run up all of those steps right up to the surface, now that she was untied, only to find the door at the top to be locked and probably impossible to break down without making a sound.

She was now leaning up against the invisible side of the Train, feeling a small sense of comfort knowing it was safe and right there behind her. She folded her arms and whistled *Jingle Bells* to herself. Evie was not the best whistler. Her attempt sounded more like puffing with the odd out-of-tune note making its way into a sound wave here and there—sometimes two in a row.

When she'd reached about the third chorus, she heard a sound way way up at the top of the steps. Surely the door must have been opened up there for her to hear noises.

Then, straining her ears to hear, she thought she could make out footsteps. Her whistling petered out all together and when she was sure that they were footsteps—one *pit* after another *pat* down the steps, she ran over to where she had been tied up, sat down on the ground and put her hands up over her head, pretending she hadn't escaped at all—just in case she could trick him.

As the footsteps continued down the stairs, they naturally became louder. Each step was ever-so-slightly more audible than the last, and the slowness of it, made the suspense for Evelyn almost unbearable.

The Captain finally came to a road, and although it looked rugged and very hilly, it would see him right into Jerusalem, where apparently his Unique Radio-Wave-Operated Link Chip was directing him.

After a long, hard hike, (and not to mention a long hard wish that he had Elisha's other horse), he was able to look out over part of the city. From what he could tell, he'd approached it this time from a northern direction—caused evidently by all the traveling around in the wilderness. He glanced down at the device in his hand and felt chuffed at being able to use it again.*

Then he looked up at the road ahead of him. It led down into a deep ravine and then wound around some flatter hills and eventually into civilization. He gave his Link-Chip device a little kiss and then set forth along the rough road—his foot obliviously stepping past a humble cluster of undergrowth beside the road. Dark green, with a strange tinge of velvety purple on its tiny little leaves.

---

* He'd only ever had to use it once before and that was shortly after he had acquired it. The event took place in 5492 A.D. and it was a strange affair involving a deck of cards, an industrial crushing machine and a dodgy boat license.

Chapter Seventeen

Getting Acquainted

No, thought Evie. If she waited here like this, pretending her arms were still tied up, she would be defenseless. What if Marius came down here in a fit of rage and went straight for her throat. In fact he probably would as soon as he found out she'd tampered with his machine. She couldn't just sit here waiting for him.

She quickly hopped up onto her feet again, the footsteps on the stairs falling into rhythm with her thumping heart beat. She darted around the dark room, looking for something to arm herself with. A stick, a log, a piece of machine equipment . . . a frying pan, a cricket bat . . .

There was nothing. She thought of the spade inside the Train that she'd used to shovel fuel into the furnace at the Captain's order. *If only I had a key!*

She was striding around the machine, desperately looking . . . A chair! There was a chair. It wasn't the best weapon of self-defense for it didn't look all that sturdy, but it would have to do.

As the footsteps grew louder every second, Evie positioned herself against the wall, beside the bottom step. She flattened herself as much as she could up against the jagged stone wall, holding the chair up above her head. She was sweating, and the butterflies inside her stomach were spreading all over her body, making her legs feel weak.

She visualized it in her mind. Actually smacking the chair down on his head—hard enough to knock him out. Then she'd make a run for it, try and find the Captain. But she started to worry about whether she could actually do it—actually harm someone enough to knock them out of consciousness. She wasn't questioning her strength, she was questioning her toughness. She'd never deliberately harmed anyone physically before. Could she do it?

As it happened, she didn't get anymore time to think it over. She had to act now, for Marius had reached the bottom step. As soon as she saw the tip of his sandal land on the ground, she stepped forward, gathered all of her strength and brought the chair down on top of his head as hard as she could. She winced, almost imagining the pain on her own head, and then watched Marius tumble to the ground. She gasped for breath immediately. She knew that it was self-defense but somehow, she still felt that sickly, guilty feeling deep in her gut.

Run. The next step in her little plan was *run*. But for some reason she didn't straight away. I think it was because she was stunned for a few seconds at what she had just done. But a bigger shock was yet to come. Marius never actually stopped moving down there on the floor. He had let out a little grunt on the impact, but now he was pushing himself back onto his feet and Evie had just lost her chance to get away. She still tried to, however it was a feeble attempt. Marius had been quick to grab her wrist and he held on to it so tightly, Evie almost lost all feeling in her hand.

It was a reflex of Evie to say "Let me go!!" but she knew there was no reason why he would let go. With his free hand, he grabbed the chair she was holding and threw it across the room. It missed his machine but hit something hard—and it wasn't the wall.

"You wretched girl!" he growled. "Did you think you could conquer me with the strength of your puny arms?"*

"I don't know," was what she managed to yelp.

"You're proving to be more of a nuisance to me than an aid."

"Yes! I'm a terrible nuisance! So why don't you just let me go?"

"Because you still interest me. I need to know who you are and where you're from!"

"No! I'm a nuisance! You said so yourself. You don't want me hanging around here like . . . chooks running around under your feet!"

"Girl, if I no longer needed you, I would not 'let you go' as you put it. I would simply dispose of you—*my* way." With that, he pulled out a weapon from his belt and held it in front of her face. She would have expected a knife, a whip or a rope or something—but it was a gun.

She swallowed. "Who said nuisance? I didn't," she said quickly. "I'm an aid. You need to find out who I am and where I'm from."

He suddenly frowned and didn't speak for a few seconds. His eyes slowly shifted over to where he'd thrown the chair. Then his head turned slowly, and then

---

* Evie did feel quite pleased with herself that she was able to at least knock him to the floor, even though it was the element of surprise—not the element of strength that did it.

his body turned. Still holding Evie tightly by the wrist, he said, "That chair . . . I threw it against the wall . . ." he walked over slowly, taking Evie with him. ". . . But it's here." It was lying in the middle of the room. He picked it up with his free hand, and then swept it up in one movement—and it hit something on its way through the air.

"What is that doing here?" he said in a low, angry growl.

"What? I don't see anything," she said quickly, wide-eyed, trying not to look guilty.

He lifted the chair again and jabbed it forward, hitting the invisible barrier.

"Don't, you'll scratch the paintwork!" she blurted out. "And that's very important paint!"

"I knew it," he said, with the slightest, sly smile. "This is your travel machine. It was made obvious by the clothes you were trying to conceal. And if that didn't give it away, your manner of speech would have."

"Well what about you and your gun? They're not supposed to be around yet for . . . for decades . . . *centuries*. What are you doing with that—let alone this huge machine! Where on earth are *you* from?" As she said this, she even plucked up enough courage to pick up her hands and dig them into her waist. One look at his face at that point though, caused her to put them back down by her sides.

"Although you are evidently from the twenty-first century, you do not talk like a time traveller."

"How would you know where I'm . . . I mean when I'm from?"

"I've travelled in time. That's how I know. How did you manage to materialise this machine?"

"You mean, the invisible one? I don't know I . . . just pressed a few buttons on *your* machine."

"Do you realise this is a very dangerous piece of equipment for someone who doesn't know what they're doing?"

"Yes I do realise. I nearly got blown up."

"You fool."

"What do you want with the Train anyway? What was it doing inside your machine?"

"How quaint. To call it a train, because it looks like one."

"It doesn't just look like one, it *is* one."

"You'll be well advised to remember that you are still a slave in this house. You will speak when you are spoken to and *I* will ask the questions."

"Surely I have the right to remain silent."

Marius laughed. "You stupid girl, now I *know* you're not a time traveller. Do you know *anything* about history? Slaves have no rights whatsoever. Now listen very carefully. I wish to own this piece of machinery you call the Train and I wish to use it to get away of this place and time and get my life back again. Now you will tell me who it is that the Train belongs to, you will take me to them and they will give me the secrets of how it works. Understand?"

She looked up at him with her big, dark brown eyes. "I understand the words that you're saying but . . . and this is the honest truth* . . . I can't do any of those things that you just asked me to do."

"I didn't ask you, I told you."

---

* I'm not sure what she meant by this. It's not like there's such a thing as the dishonest truth.

"But I can't. I don't even know where he is, the man who owns the Train and even if I did and I took you to him, he probably wouldn't just obey you. He's not really a person you can just order around."

"Just tell me who he is."

Evie began to sweat again. "No."

Marius raised his gun again. "You will tell me or I will kill you."

"But I'm an aid. You need to find out who I am and where I'm from."

"Been there, done that. Tell me!"

"It wouldn't mean anything to you, it's just a name."

"Then just tell me what it is."

Suddenly, a thought came to her. An honest thought. "I . . . I don't know his name."

"You lying wretch."

"It's true! I don't know what his name his, he hasn't told me!"

"You're a stupid creature. I think now would be a good time to—as the saying goes—say your prayers." He loaded the pistol.

She took in a deep breath, and had a sudden wave of courage. With her free hand, she took a swing at the gun in his hand, hoping he wasn't expecting her to do that, thus arming herself with the element of surprise again. He apparently had not expected her to take that action, and the gun went flying across the room and then skidded along the floor. She made a run for it, towards the long flight of steps, but he ran after her, grabbed her around the neck and pulled her back down. Once he'd achieved that, Evie hoped he would take his arm away from her throat, but he didn't. Soon, Evie found that she could no longer breathe. She was gasping for air but nothing was getting through to her lungs. In one terrifying moment, Evie realised that she was being strangled. She could feel his bulging bicep pressing against her neck and any attempt to pull his arm away was like trying to heave a thick tree trunk out of the ground. She tried to yell out, but nothing came except for a suppressed cough. Soon, she began to feel fuzzy in the head. Both her hearing and vision began to grow dimmer and dimmer, and so she was only vaguely conscious when she thought she could feel another presence in the room.

What happened next happened so fast that in the time taken for you to read it, it could have happened ten times over. Someone tapped Marius on the shoulder, distracting him from his murderous task and suddenly Evie dropped weakly to the floor. She managed to turn herself around to try and see what had happened and she saw two figures. One was clearly Marius and the other . . . when her eyes cleared back into focus, she realised was . . .

"Captain!" she exclaimed with joy and relief, and she rubbed her eyes to make sure she wasn't just seeing what she wanted to see.

He stood there, strong, like a knight in shining armour, but soon Marius charged for him with murder in his eyes.

As Marius came within arm's reach, the Captain said, "If that's the way you want it." He took out the Atom Relocating Molecular Teleport Device, pressed a button on it and shoved it straight into Marius' chest.

As a reflex, Marius grabbed it, the Captain let go, and in the blink of an eye, Marius was gone. The room was silent for a few seconds.

"Banishment for attempted murder, and bad breath," said the Captain, dusting off his hands.

Evie gazed up with her mouth wide open, her hands massaging her tender neck. Then the Captain walked forward and held an arm down to her, sporting a big smile.

She took his hand and he hoisted her up onto her feet. Without a word, she hugged him and failing to suppress them, tears rolled down her cheeks unashamedly.

After a while, she broke away from him. "You certainly know how to search for someone. How did you find me?"

"As a matter of fact, I haven't found what I'm looking for yet. I was looking for the Train."

"Oh, and never mind about me, huh?"

"Well you're an added bonus, of course."

"You were just in time. He was going to kill me."

"Yes, who *was* that disagreeable fellow?"

"My master technically. You see, I'm his slave. Oh there's so much to tell you but . . . wait, what's happened to him? Where's he gone?"

"I just set my Atom Relocating Molecular Teleport Device for somewhere in the Kidron Valley—not far from where Paulo and I were banished to."

"You and Paulo were banished? Gee we're doing real well here aren't we? Wait a minute, where is Paulo."

"We don't have time, I need to find the Train. My instrument led me here, which is strange. *Unless*, the Train, or more accurately, components inside the Train have some sort of telepathic ability—that the active particles inside the atmosphere inside the Train have some mysterious affect on anyone who enters it and travels in it—not enough for any damage to be done, but enough for some particles to actually get into the person's respiratory system and be absorbed into the body, creating a biochemical connection between person and Train. And therefore, in leading me to the Train, my Unique Radio-Wave-Operated Link Chip, instead, led me to you." The Captain appeared to be amazed and baffled at the same time. "I've never discovered that about her before. The Train could be even more complex than I've thought all these years."

"*Or*," Evie said, managing to finally get a word in, "perhaps the Train is here in this room, which is what possibly could have caused your instrument to lead you here." Evie knew that the Captain always kept his piloting goggles in his outside jacket pocket. She got them out for him and placed them in front of his eyes.

"Ah," said the Captain. "Good."

Paulo and Silius were busting at the seams with Violet-Assassin-Fighting fruit, their brows absolutely dripping with perspiration.

"Hey Silius, I've been thinking," said Paulo, catching his breath, "Shouldn't we try this out before we exhaust ourselves completely on this endeavour? We could make a small batch of juice with what we've got, take it to a patch of the stuff and see if it works."

"You didn't just take the Captain's word for it?"

"Well he was only guessing."

"I was hoping you had more faith in him than that. I, too, was thinking the same thing."

"It's not that I don't have faith in him, but he said he had no idea whether it would work and that it's worth a try. Well we need to try it now."

"I agree."

"Now where was that big patch of it?"

"About a hundred yards that way, I recall."

"Come on."

Shortly, they came to the spot, and they got as close to the line of vegetation as they dared.

"Well now that we're here," said Silius, "how are we going to juice them?"

"With our hands."

"I meant what are we going to juice them *into*?"

Paulo put his thinking cap on. He looked at Silius, about to tell him 'I don't know', but (speaking of caps) he suddenly noticed Silius' helmet. It was like a round bowl upside-down on top of his head, with the bright red feathery brush thing sticking out the top. "Your helmet," said Paulo. "Would you mind terribly if we juiced the fruit into there? Or is that against the law?"✲

Realising the obviousness of the solution, Silius took it straight off and said, "Yes, of course! I mean, no, I don't mind, let's do it."

They squashed up four or five of the fruits with their hands into the helmet. It was quite clumsily done, but good enough to serve their purpose. They wasted no time, once there was a good amount of runny pinky-orangey juice, they poured it over a small surface area of the plant and waited.

There was a small reaction. Eventually it went a slightly different colour, but after that, they waited for

---

✲   It could very well have been. In the Roman soldier rule book, right after 'do not be cheerful to passers by' and just before 'be sure to mention Caesar when anyone asks thou who thouest barrack for' it might say 'thou must not juice fruit inside thine helmet.

more to happen. Nothing did. They could have sat there all day and night and nothing would have happened.

"Do you think maybe it's taken out the toxicity?" asked Silius, doubtfully.

"How do you feel about testing that theory?" Paulo said, also doubtfully.

"You are right. We'll never know. What do we do now?"

"Look!" Paulo said suddenly, pointing at the plant that had been soaked in fruit juice. But it wasn't an optimistic 'look' at all. What he had observed, was the leaves of the plant slowly returning to their original colour. As if it had a built in defense mechanism and was repelling any trace of the juice.

"It hasn't worked," said Paulo, almost in disbelief. "It hasn't worked."

Chapter Eighteen

The Captain's Secret Adventure

"So it was *me* that saved my life?" said Evie, stepping up onto an invisible step.

"Yes, you switching on this ridiculous over-sized machine and bringing the Train back into space and time was what brought me here. Before that, I couldn't get a signal for the Train, because it didn't exist."

"But what *is* that machine?"

"Well you tell me. You're the one who's tinkered around with it," said the Captain, now entering the Train.

"All I did was push a few buttons," she said, hopping on after him.

"Just start by telling me what you know."

"Well there was a black button, and a red button, and one of them was a self-destruct button, which I pressed and nearly got blown up, and the other button released the Train from 'the vortex' it said. And there was an 'on' button, which turned it on . . ."

"And an 'off' button, which turned it off?" the Captain said looking down at his controls.

"I think that was the same button as the 'on' button. Oh and one button I pressed brought up an image of the

Train. Assumedly when it was still *in the vortex.*" She said the last three words in a low, mystical voice.

"Interesting," said the Captain. Although, he didn't appear to be concentrating on what Evie was saying at all.

A picture came up on a small screen on the Train's control deck. It looked like an Internet page.

"What are you doing? Googling something?"

"Precisely." He typed in some words.

Evie read them out as he did, "Kra . . . til . . . lia . . . loo . . . lumis. What's that?"

"Something that is very possibly endangering the whole population of Jerusalem in the future and right now, today."

"Huh? I thought as soon as we'd found the Train, we could just . . . leave."

"Evelyn, why do you suppose that man had a gun?"

"Cause he's mean? He's definitely one nasty piece-a work."

"Wrong. Because he's not from this time."

"Oh yeah, I already knew that."

"And what's more, he knows you're from a different time too."

"Yeah he does. But how did you know?"

The Captain looked at Evie and glanced up and down at her attire.

"Oh yeah. The robe came off when he tried to whip me. What happened to yours?"

"It was hot out in that valley. Did you say he whipped you?"

"No, he was about to. But I ran. But he caught me. But I escaped. But then he found me. But then *you* found me! And now here . . . wait a second, if you zapped him

172

out to the . . . whatever it is you said, well now he's got your what-sa-ma-call-it teleport thing. He could go anywhere he wants to and you'll never get it back! What did you do that for?"

"It won't work again for another twenty-four hours yet. And trust me, he'll be wanting to head straight back here, mark my words."

"Well I don't know. You're losing me, I'm getting real confused now. Especially with this new development, this Kratilia Loo Loo thing."

"On the contrary. Put that together with the man with the gun, and it's all finally starting to make sense."

"Well then you must know something I don't."

"I know a lot of things you don't know, but that's not the point."

"Wait a second, the coin."

"What coin?"

"I found this coin and it did not belong here. Get this, it was a coin with ONE SHILLING written on it. And it looked like a picture of some English king."

"Ah."

"Except, I thought Marius must have been from the far future. I mean a further future than where I'm from because of that hi-tech machine. But you can't tell me shillings will be in the currency for that long."

"Mmm," said the Captain. "Have you got this coin now?"

"No, Callista snatched it back. She was a slave that I worked with. She's the one who actually found it. She just thought it was pretty."

"Did you hear that?" the Captain said all of a sudden.

"What?"

173

"Someone calling out. Are there any other slaves here?"

"No, just me. There used to be Levi, but he got sold by Marius along with some shekels or something to buy me. Marius must have already been suspicious of me back then, he was dead set on having me as his own slave."

"So there's no one else in the house?"

"Um . . . oh, Marius' wife could be."

"Marius' *wife*?" The Captain seemed confused.

"*Marius!!*"

"I heard it that time," said Evie. "Yeah, that's Portia, Marius' wife. Sounds like she's coming down. She'll see everything!"

"You'd better go and look after her."

"What do I say to her?"

"Tell her . . . tell her . . . I don't know, tell her something."

"Okay. Mistress, I'm sorry but your husband has been broken up into millions of tiny atoms and reassembled in the . . . the . . ."

"Kidron Valley."

"The Kidron Valley. Oh don't cry, Mistress, I'm sure it's only temporary. How does that sound?"

"Fine. Fine," he said, seeming again not to be paying any attention to what she was saying.

Evie, giving a little sigh of frustration, left the engine room, left the Train and entered back into the dull underground chamber, soon finding an extremely baffled Portia on the bottom step.

She looked speechless, but she said something. "What *is* going *on* here?"

"I . . . don't really know," said Evie.

"Where's my husband? I can't find him anywhere."

"I don't know . . . exactly."

"Then what good are you?" she said, walking into the middle of the room. "What is this thing?" she said, looking up at the machine.

"I . . . don't know."

Portia's angry eyes locked down onto Evie's wide, innocent eyes. "You don't know much, do you? I can tell you what it is *not*."

"What's that?"

"It is *not* a birthday present. That, I can be sure of."

"Is that what he told you?"

"That is none of your concern."

"Please, let's get one thing straight," she tried to say politely, "I'm not a slave."

"Yes you are. My husband paid good money for you, of course you are, you stupid, inferior girl."

"I got a 'B minus' in maths last term, I am *not* stupid."

"What are these nonsense babblings? Now find your master for me, I order it."

"But . . . I can't."

"You can't?" she said, temper rising.

"I can't without actually leaving the city."

"Explain yourself."

"Well, you see he went. . . . out . . . of the house . . . and . . . listen, haven't you been wondering where I was and why the chores haven't been done in the house? I've been locked up down here. Marius tied me up!"

"If you had done something to displease him, then he was right to. I can't think why he wanted to buy you from Lucius. You're completely useless."

"Portia, we think your husband . . ."

"You test my patience, addressing me this way."

175

"Well it *is* your name, isn't it?" Evie was losing *her* patience a little bit. "Look your husband, we think is . . . from another world. Another time, in fact." Then Evie had a horrible thought. "Unless," she swallowed, "you're in on it with him."

"*In on it,* what are you raving about?"

Evie had a slight feeling of relief, perceiving her to be earnest. "You're never going to listen to me as long as you see me as a slave, are you," she mumbled.

Just then, there was a loud sound in the room. Evie could hardly believe her ears. It was the sound of the Train!

chuff *choofety chuff, choofety*
chuff *choofety BANG! choofety*
chuff *choofety chuff, choofety*
chuff *choofety BANG . . .*

"Captain!" she yelled out, and ran to the space where the Train was supposed to be. The sound was fading. "No!" She reached out to grab the door of the Train, but was terrified to realise her body had just plummeted straight through to the stone wall behind it. The Train was no longer there.

"Captain," she said softly, "don't leave me here."

"I hope the Captain finds the Train," said Paulo, wiping the sweat from his brow.

"What is a Train?" said Silius.

Paulo looked up slowly, "You're not going to believe me but here goes . . . it's a spaceship."

"What's a spaceship?"

"Er, um . . ." Paulo was taken off guard. "A . . . mode of transport . . . that travels through space."

"That's nothing new. Do not all modes of transport travel through space?"

"You're right. No this one, um, travels in outer space. Amongst the stars and the planets."

Silius was quiet for a moment. He then had a confused sort of smile—looking at Paulo as if he was nuts. "That is not possible."

"Well, it also travels through time and we're from the future and in the future . . . it *is* possible . . . I guess."

He was quiet again for another moment. ". . . I had no idea."

Paulo smiled.

Silius continued, "I had no idea, that for approximately the last hour, I have been walking around with a lunatic."

"What? Well where do you think this plant comes from then if not from another world?"

"All your friend said was that it came from somewhere a little further away than another city. Now I do not know how big the Earth is, but there must be many different lands and countries besides the Middle East."

"Okay," Paulo said, surrendering. "Okay, never mind. Look, what are we going to do about the plant?"

"There's nothing we can do. The juice of the fruit does not work, we have no other orders from your friend as to what action to take next . . ."

"So the fruit, or probably anything native only cures the *effects* of the plant once it's poisoned someone, while not having any effect on the plant itself."

"Yes. So what do you propose we do?"

"No idea. I vote we look for Evie. Another friend of mine who could be in trouble."

"Another one of these lunatics, no doubt."

"You'll be able to get us back to the city, won't you?"

"Yes."

"Well let's do that."

"Are you sure that we should? The Captain won't know where to find us again."

"It's better than feeling absolutely useless. Anyway he said he'd meet us at the palace eventually. Come on, let's both get back on the horse and get out of here."

And so they did—leaving giant patches of the Violet Assassin untreated, and slowly spreading.

Evie was staring in sheer disbelief at the empty space in front of her♣ and she was absolutely dumbfounded.

"Are you out of your mind?" intruded the voice of Portia all of sudden. "Come here immediately."

Evie did as she was told.

"Now, I want a straight answer from you. What is this monstrosity, and what has happened to my husband?"

"Has your husband been secretive a lot?"

"I demand you answer my questions."

"Does he sometimes disappear down here and you don't see him for hours and hours?"

Portia then, started listening.

"Does he sometimes use words that you don't understand or even patronise you a little?"

She was silent.

♣ Even though if the Train *was* there, she'd still be staring at an empty space.

"I can tell by your expression that I'm right. Ever wondered why?"

"My husband is a good man. He loves me and . . . we have no secrets." Her voice trailed off and lost its convincing edge.

"How well do you really know him though?"

"I will not put up with this impudence!"

"I don't even know what that means,* but I'm trying to help you!"

"I do not need to be helped. My marriage is as strong as . . . as strong as . . ." she appeared to weaken, ". . . No one has ever noticed those things . . . just me . . . I've been the only one. I haven't been able to talk to anyone about it and when I tried to, no one would believe me."

This time, Evie listened.

"He puts on an act. Sometimes in front of me, but mostly in front of other people. He pretends to be the nicest, most considerate husband you could ever meet and it makes me sick because he's not. A lot of my life is . . . is miserable. But it's not only that. There's something else about him, something . . . something . . ."

"Something different. Like he doesn't belong here."

"Yes, but he was like that more when I first met him. Not so much now."

"As if now, he's blending in more and more the longer he's here." The whole situation was sinking in to Evelyn at the same time as she was trying to explain it to Portia.

"So, he's from a different part of the world. What is so unusual about that?"

"But he calls himself a Roman doesn't he?"

---

*   It means impertinence, cheek, disrespect, impoliteness.

"Yes. Well . . . I assumed it from the beginning. He did not tell me otherwise."

"Ah *ha*!"

"What?"

Evie's shoulders sank. "I don't know, really. You ought to talk to the Captain. He'd be able to tell you exactly what's going on."

"Just what exactly are you trying to tell me," Portia said, her anger returning slightly. "That my husband is a dangerous man? That he's been living a lie all these eight years? . . . That he doesn't love me?"

"Well, I don't know about that . . . but I think you're right about him living a lie. And I think that definitely he's a dangerous man."

All of a sudden, Evie thought she heard the Train again. It was faint, but it was quickly getting louder and louder—getting nearer, until suddenly it stopped. Relief came over Evie and she ran straight over to the corner of the room, holding her arms out in front of her, feeling for the Train's side. But before she reached it, the Captain came bursting out of the door, panting like crazy and covered in dirt and sweat. His clothes were torn and dishevelled and he could barely stand on his own two feet. In fact, when he emerged from the Train, he practically collapsed into Evie's arms.

Chapter Nineteen

The Trickster's Easy Prey

Silius was making good time on the horse. Paulo was admiring the animal's strength and speed, and beauty. He felt it was a shame it had to wear all the reins and saddle and harnesses and baskets and blankets. He remembered seeing the Roman horses around the palace of King Herod and all the gear they had to wear and felt sorry for them. He imagined how much nobler they would look without all of that palaver. Paulo was also admiring Silius' horse-riding skill. He seemed to do it effortlessly.

Quite soon, the pair of them could see the hills surrounding the city. "We'll be there in a few minutes now," said Silius.

Then straight after that, they heard a distant voice, calling. "Hello! Stop please!"

Silius stopped the horse and looked for the owner of the voice. Not far away, was a man waving his arms, then starting to run over to Paulo and Silius.

"Hark!" he called, "I need assistance! I'm stranded out here and I need to get back to my house just on the edge of Jerusalem." He was a stocky man, short black hair with a short beard, wearing Roman clothes. He looked ordinary enough, except he was holding something, which Paulo found very interesting.

"We are on our way to the city," said Silius, as the man reached the horse's side. "How did you come to be stranded out here?"

"I don't know, exactly . . . wait, I know you," the man said, looking at Silius, starting to smile. "Silous is it? Sirion?"

"Silius."

"Yes, that's right. You're a soldier in the king's regiment."

"Yes . . . ?"

"So am I. I'm Marius. We've worked beside each other in the past, I'm sure of it."

"Oh yes, Marius! I do remember you. I didn't recognise you without your uniform."

"I'm on leave at the moment."

Paulo had been sitting on the horse, just staring at the box Marius held in his hand. It looked a lot like the Captain's Atom Relocating Molecular Teleport Device.

Marius noticed that it was being stared at and he looked Paulo up and down. "Who is your friend?"

"This is Paulo a . . . a new friend of mine I suppose."

"What is he, a Jew?"

"Er . . . I don't know," he said, looking at Paulo.

"Never mind," said Marius, starting to get suspicious of the boy. He didn't look like a Jew. Nor a Roman. Marius smiled suddenly. What Paulo and Silius unfortunately did not know at the time, was that it was a manufactured smile. A fake.

"May I ask," said Paulo, "how did you come by that . . . strange looking object you have there?" He tried to sound like someone who'd never seen anything like it before.

But it was too late. Marius had already detected in his face that Paulo was allied with Evelyn and the man who'd rescued her and sent him out into the wilderness in the process.

To Paulo's surprise, Marius replied in a somewhat more hushed and secretive voice, "It is a teleport device your friend lent to me to get you out of here. I'm sure you're familiar with it."

"A teleport device?" said Silius. "What on earth is a teleport device?"

"I don't understand it either," Marius said with apparent wonderment, "but your friend . . . the one you call *Captain* used it to send me out here to find you."

Paulo, at first, looked confused.

"He figured if you were journeying back by yourselves, you'd never find each other in a big city like Jerusalem. That's why he sent me. I can take you right to him."

Marius could tell Paulo wasn't pleased in the way he expected him to be.

"What is troubling you?"

"Well it's not the Captain I'm worried about. I was going to look for Evie. She got taken . . ."

"Evie?" Marius interrupted, his face lighting up suddenly. "The Captain *found* Evie, they're together now."

"Really?"

"Yes! So come on! I'll take you to them. There's no time to lose. They need your help."

"For what? What's happening?"

"I do not know, I'm just passing on what he said." Marius grabbed the reins of the horse and led them into the city of Jerusalem himself.

It was only a slightly better experience riding in the front of a chariot than it was riding in the back. Although it was probably only because now she knew she wasn't alone anymore, and because the Captain gave her turns at steering the horse.

After the Captain had collapsed into her arms, Evie had noticed a small glass bottle filled with a bright yellow syrupy liquid that was clutched in his hand. He explained nothing. All he said was that they had to skedaddle. He had locked up the Train and asked Portia if they could borrow her and Marius' chariot to skedaddle on. Meanwhile, all this time, Portia had been asking question after question about what was going on. With no time to explain, the Captain gave her a chance to skedaddle with them, but she chose to stay in the house and wait for Marius to appear. She was in a terrible state and Evie felt bad, not being able to stay with her, explain to her, and reassure her. It was quite amazing that she let Evie go. I think she was in such a state of shock and confusion, that a dancing bear could've waltzed through the room and she wouldn't have noticed.

Anyway, that all having happened so quickly, Evie now had a chance to actually enjoy this chariot ride with the Captain. She even chuckled to herself when she thought of her friends at school—and if only they could see her now.

"Haven't you got questions for me whizzing around in your head?" the Captain said, breaking the silence.

"What, you want me to actually ask them?"

"Sure, go ahead."

"Okay. Um . . . what's in the bottle? Where are we going? Where's Paulo (as I recall asking earlier), where have you been just now? And what is that brown stuff on your face?"

"Let me see now . . . Yellow-venomed flat-top snake venom, around and about, near the Kidron Valley, somewhere to get the yellow-venomed flat-top snake venom, and mud."

"What?"

"Okay, it's not mud, it's Camazonian Bat poo, but they're very hygienic creatures so . . ."

"No I mean, what do you mean by around and about? We're not actually *going* anywhere?"

"Correct. We're looking for . . . ah-ha." The Captain stopped mid-sentence as if he'd spotted something. He stopped the chariot, jumped off and ran over to a nearby tree.

"Bat poo?" Evie said, hopping off after him, "That's disgusting!"

This wasn't a very busy part of town. And it was just as well, Evie thought, because whatever the Captain was doing, looked rather suspicious.

Evie decided to walk over and watch what he was doing. He squatted down in front of a small patch of dark purpley-green plant growth, took a cork stopper off the top of the bottle he was holding and then said with an air of hopefulness, "Here come old flat-top," and he poured the tiniest drop of the bright yellow liquid onto the very edge of a small leaf growing out of the ground.

Before her very eyes, the strangest thing happened. To the Captain, it was evidently what was supposed to happen and he was quietly elated by it. The leaves, within no time at all started curling up at the edges and then shriveling up altogether. The effect grew—spreading out from the affected spot to the rest of the plant. In about seven seconds, the whole plant was clearly dead. The Captain then rustled up the soil with his gardening-gloved hand and the roots finding surface were black like charcoal and still in their process of shriveling up into nothing—like a thread of cotton to a flame.

"Success," said the Captain, breathing relief finally.

"Okay," said Evie, staring at the ground, "Please explain?"

The Captain put the cork back on the bottle and answered, "The plant is called Kratilier Lumis and it's deadly."

As a reflex, Evie quickly snatched her fingers away and held them behind her back.

The Captain explained the whole scenario to her. "The venomous snake lives in the same, tropical jungle habitat as the plant. The ecosystem has been created so perfectly, that the plant can do its job, but without growing out of control because of the presence of the yellow venomed flat-top snake. It's the only thing that can kill the plant apparently."

"That's amazing."

"*God* is amazing, yes. There's similarly amazing things like this in every ecosystem. That's how ecosystems work."

"But . . . how did the plant get here in the first place?"

"Have a think."

Only after a few seconds did Evie's face light up. "Marius! He must have brought it over with him—from wherever he's from. Where *is* he from?"

"That's not what's important now. What's important is that there's who-knows-how-many more patches of this stuff here, there and everywhere around Jerusalem. Perhaps even beyond."

"But how has it spread?"

"On people's shoes, horses, chariots."

"But it'd be *everywhere!*"

"Fortunately, the Violet Assassin doesn't always take root—it's a difficult plant to get growing."♣ He stood up and started walking back to the chariot.

"So we're literally just riding around looking for Violet Assassin to kill?"

"Quite literally, yes. Off we go then."

Evie hopped on after the Captain and they took off again with their eyes peeled.

Marius knew the city well. It didn't take him long to find his way back to his own village where his own little house lay and where his own little wife was waiting.

"I don't think I've ever been so glad to see civilization in my life," said Paulo, as they passed more and more people going about their business.

"My house is not much further," said Marius, and once they'd arrived, Portia came running out, demanding answers from her husband. He didn't answer. All he said was 'not now, woman' and led Paulo and Silius straight down to the room downstairs, (on his way, noticing that his horse and chariot were gone.)

"This is where they were," said Marius, breathlessly and with a tone of urgency. "They were here in this room, I don't understand."

"What did the Captain tell you?" said Paulo.

♣ For any of you budding gardeners out there. It needs full sunlight and not a lot of water. Does not survive in cold environments but can grow well in dry or damp. Needs minimal drainage.

"He said he'd wait for us. They should be here . . . they must have been taken."

"Taken?"

"Kidnapped. They must be in terrible trouble."

"Kidnapped by whom?"*

"I don't know. The Captain spoke of some foreign character—some person from another world he said—who was after his . . . train?"

"The Train?" cried Paulo, falling right into the trap.

"That's what he said. He also mentioned something about a secret headquarters. Underneath the temple of Jerusalem, where this person, or persons are hiding—making their plans."

"Could it be where they've taken Evie and the Captain?"

"I don't know, but I'd say that's a good guess."

"Do you know where this temple is?"

"Of course."

"We both do," said Silius.

"Well we should go there, and not waste any time," said Paulo. "Is it far? Do we have transport?"

"You would have a chariot of your own wouldn't you, Marius?" said Silius.

"Yes . . . yes, *that's* how they would have got away. As we were approaching the house, I noticed that my chariot was not there." Marius was pacing across the floor as he was talking. Now everything he'd been saying down in that room so far, had been quite frankly, a load of rubbish, and when he came over towards the far side of the room and deliberately/*accidentally* walked into a large

---

* Paulo actually said 'who', but he should've said 'whom' to be grammatically correct.

hard object that wasn't there, he managed to generate some more deception, "What's this?"

When Paulo realised Marius was looking up at nothing, but convinced that something was there, his face lit up and he said, "The Train!"

Marius was smiling inside. That stupid girl, Evie had done him a favour by pulling the Train out of the vortex. "The train, as in the Train the Captain spoke of?"

"Yes!" Paulo said, coming over and feeling it with his hands. "We could use this . . ." then his enthusiasm dropped, ". . . if we knew how to operate it."

"Operate it? We have to get into the thing first," Marius said.

"I don't understand," said Silius, "I don't see anything!"♣

"This is the Captain's spaceship I was telling you about. Feel." He put Silius' hand out so that it touched the smooth metal paneling. Paulo needed no more encouragement from Marius. He reached into one of his overall pockets and pulled out a long thin wiry object of non-descript shape. "If I can just get inside, I might be able to figure out the mechanics. Setting the coordinates for our destination shouldn't be too hard." Paulo was poking at the space with the small object—twisting it around and jiggling it back and forth. It was a lock-pick. An essential item for Satellite workers to always have on hand apparently.♦

♣ An unfortunate part of the story here is that Paulo missed a vital clue. If he stopped and thought for a second or two, he would have realised that this is what Marius should have been saying too.

♦ As one of his colleagues, Squirt also had one on him which got him, the Captain and Evelyn out of a sticky situation.

As Marius patiently watched and waited, Paulo manipulated the lock with his pick, starting to think that the Captain would have been cleverer than to put a lock on his Train that could easily be picked open; and Silius was still in a quandary as to what was going on.

Then soon, there was a *click* and then a door-openingy sound. (It was a very good lock-pick.) Paulo could see the interior of the Train. He walked in and was followed by one baffled Roman, and another pretending-to-be-baffled pretend-Roman.

However, once they were all in and Paulo had closed the outer door, Marius no longer made an effort to appear the baffled, helping, citizen of Jerusalem.

Chapter Twenty

Wanna Bet?

"So what exactly are we fighting here?" asked Evie as they destroyed their second lot of Violet Assassin. "The plant? Marius? Can't be another blue blob can it?"

"The plant is merely a symptom of the greater problem," the Captain replied. "I believe it's Marius who is the problem."

"But what does he want?"

"It would seem that he wants the Train."

"Is that it? Not world domination. Not to take over the minds of these 'primitives'?"

"Certainly not. I think all he wants to do is get away from them."

"Hence attempting to steal the Train. *Transport.*"

"Exactly."

"So if he had transport . . ."

"We're talking intergalactic transport."

". . . Then he'd be happy and leave everyone alone?"

"Well . . ."

"He could just hitch a ride with us."

"Mmm . . ."

"I mean, he's thoroughly unpleasant, but you're into blessing people even if they do wrong aren't you. It's what the Bible says."

"Evie, I'm not sure if it's as simple as that. Something tells me he's going to want what I can't give him. He doesn't want a ride. He wants the freedom to travel around indefinitely."

"He might not."

"Alright, he might not. But I'd be prepared to put my money on it."

"How much?"

"No, I don't *actually* want to bet."

"You're not very confident then, are you." Evie put her tongue in her cheek.

"It's a figure of speech. I'm one hundred percent certain, but I'm not fond of gambling. So let's go, we've got a lot to do."

"What's that big huge building over there?" Evie said, pointing.

The Captain looked up. "That's the temple. Don't you look at the illustrations in the back of your Bible?"

"The *actual* temple of Jerusalem?"

"Yep. And that's where we're heading next. Come on."

There was a ***chuff*** *choofety chuffing* resonating around the underground room of Marius' house and in the engine room of the Train, things were rattling around with the motion of the engine firing up. Paulo was smiling and in the shadows, in a corner of the room, Marius was smiling too.

"That's got it started," Paulo said. "To be honest, I thought it'd be harder. Now, how can I find a map of this city?" he said to himself.

Marius could see the keyboard on the front control panel beneath the big front window—he knew there must be an inbuilt databank. He made a decision, walked over, examined the controls for half-a-minute and then started pressing buttons.

"What are you doing?" Paulo asked.

First, Marius said, "I'm looking up the coordinates for the Temple of Jerusalem."

"How do you know how to do that?"

Marius didn't say anything. Paulo stepped over. "That's not Jerusalem," Paulo realised. "That's . . . that's not even Earth! What are you doing?" He grabbed Marius' arm—mainly in order to see over his shoulder.

Marius raised up his power-house arm and it knocked Paulo back against the wall.

"Marius, what is going on?" Silius asked. "Are you to pretend you understand all this . . . this, this machinery?"

"I do understand it, you fool." He locked in a setting of coordinates and turned around to face the others. "Thanks to this gullible, lock-picking air-head, I have what I've wanted and needed for eight long years. I am now free to do as *I* wish, to go where *I* please! It won't take me long to decipher how to fly this machine myself, and when I do, I won't be needing either of you anymore."

"But . . . what about the Captain and Evie?" Paulo said, sounding like an idiot.

"And what about your wife?" said Silius.

Marius laughed. "You're both as *silius* as each other. My life here was no more than a disguise. An inflicted circumstance from which I've been trying to get away, these past eight years. *And no one can stop me now!*" He pulled a lever and the Train bounded into action.

"Hullo, what's this?" said the Captain all of a sudden. They had almost reached the Temple, but had to stop nearby, where a construction project appeared to be underway.

"What?"

There was beeping from the Captain's pocket. He pulled out his Unique Radio-Wave Operated Link-Chip and it was flashing.

"Someone's using the Train."

"How can that be," she asked with emerging alarm.

"I don't know. Perhaps I shouldn't have left it there unattended."

"I think *definitely* you shouldn't have left it unatten . . ."

"Wait a second, wait a second, don't panic. Whoever's driving won't get far, look, I can do something specky. Watch." And he turned one of the knobs on the device and waved it around up in the air like you would with a mobile phone to get reception.

Right at that moment, there was a big clunk and a jolt, which shook the whole Train. Suddenly, Marius was being told by the controls that the ship was making an emergency materialisation.

"No! What's going on?" He turned to Paulo, threatening him suddenly with a dagger from his belt. "What have you done?"

"I haven't done anything! I promise!"

Soon, the Train stopped making so much noise, and everything was still.

The Captain put the Link-Chip away and pulled out his glasses. Hopping out of the chariot, he put them on and Evie watched him walk boldly away. Soon, she guessed it was the Train he was approaching, and then her idea was confirmed when she saw a big tough Roman step out of thin air. She knew straight away it was Marius. She was thrilled all of a sudden to see Paulo come out after him. But to her horror, Marius was holding a knife to his neck.

The Captain, on the other hand, kept his emotions private. Up until now, he had only brushed shoulders with the enemy, but now, it seemed they were going to have a proper talk. Hostage negotiation, was one of the Captain's most dreaded tasks.

Both Paulo and Evie looked terrified. The Captain tried to keep everyone calm. He started by asking, "Where is Silius, Paulo?"

Paulo's face was a picture of absolute sadness as well as terror. The Captain swallowed. "You haven't," he said with disgust to Marius.

"I began to dispose of unnecessary baggage on board my ship, but when I realised my plans were going to be interfered with, I thought I'd keep this one alive to use as a bargaining chip."

"I don't like gambling much," said the Captain.

Marius smiled. "Then simply allow me to commandeer your spacecraft and no one else will be hurt."

Ignoring this, the Captain said, "So what's your real name by the way. 'Marius' is so uncannily Roman and you're clearly not. I'd like to know who I'm going to be handing my Train over to."

"Mallory if you must know. I don't know my last name, since I was an orphan from birth. But you don't want to hear my life's sob story."

"Certainly not, thank you. Why do you want my Train?"

"I don't belong here. I want to leave. I've wanted to leave for eight long years."

"I thought we agreed no sob stories. Why didn't you leave the way you came?"

Mallory gave a short bitter chuckle. "If only it was that easy. I was abandoned here. It was my partner who built the machine and it was to be our freedom back then. It was more or less a teleport machine, but it could only teleport one person at a time, taking years of work to prepare it for another trip. It's the best we could do with such primitive resources. My partner decided he no longer needed me and took off without me. I damaged it in my rage when he left, and since then, I've been repairing it, improving it, enhancing its features so that it can pull objects as well as people into the vortex and out again. When I detected your craft in the vortex, I seized the opportunity. You see I never again got it to teleport a person to a precise destination as before. It's more of a collector now. It finds things and rips them out of the vortex and rematerialises them beside the machine. So there was no way I could find my own salvation in it. But it could *bring* my salvation to *me*."

"Who is this partner of yours? And how did you get here in the first place?"

"You don't know? Surely you would have worked it out . . . But I don't suppose it really matters in the scheme of things. I simply followed the leader. And look where it got me."

"What's that supposed to mean?"

"Are you giving me the Train or not?"

"Don't, Captain!" cried Paulo, and Marius tightened his grip on him.

"Would you accept a lift somewhere?" asked the Captain, knowing what the answer would be, but merely asking it to satisfy Evie.

"I want a permanent form of transport, Captain Dumbo. I want to have the freedom to travel anywhere, any time. There's no way I'm going to be content to stay in one galaxy *all* of my life."

"See," the Captain turned around and told Evie. "At least I tried."

"Sometimes we don't always get what we want!" shouted Evie, not knowing herself. "That's life!"

The Captain, still looking at her, raised his eyebrows in surprise. He was proud of her for being brave enough to shout at him, but he said softly to her, "Usually men with knives at your friend's neck get what they want, Evelyn."

Evie shut her mouth at that, content now to stay quiet.

"Well?" Mallory shouted, with growing impatience.

"What's in it for me?" said the Captain.

Evie and Paulo were both shocked at this question.

"Your friend doesn't die, and you don't get the horrible job of cleaning up the mess I made in there." He glanced back inside the Train and said sarcastically, "Alas poor Silius, I knew him well."

The Captain closed his eyes in regret for what had apparently happened to Silius. He could tell by Paulo's face that it wasn't a bluff.

"I want more in return than just my friend's life and . . . the other you mentioned. I want my Atom Relocating Molecular Teleport Device back."

"What this?" Mallory pulled it out of his pocket, smiling mockingly. "Alright if you wish. But I won't give it to you until I have your guarantee I can fly away in this thing."

"Captain, what are you doing?" cried Evie.

"Life is very short," the Captain told her, then he turned back to Mallory, "and there's no time for fussing and fighting my friend. It's a deal."

"Captain no!" yelled Paulo.

"Right," said Mallory, not giving up the teleport device just yet. He looked around at their surroundings. "This is quite a convenient spot, Captain. See that cistern?"

The Captain had been aware that there was one there.* "Yes," he replied.

"That's where you're going. Because I don't trust you to just let me disappear. I know you."

"How do you know me?"

---

* A cistern, as you and I know it, is the little tank of water that sits above the toilet seat. It holds the water that flushes everything away once you've 'been' and then fills up again with water for the next time the toilet is in use. In ancient times, a cistern was similarly, a water supply; however it stored a much bigger amount of water. It was a large concrete tank built beneath the ground, to supply water for a whole area or small village—for bathing, washing, and sometimes drinking. This particular cistern was very old and brittle and wasn't being used anymore. The ground had been dug up a little around it, revealing the opening, so it looked like a large, old, underground cellar.

". . . You'd probably have some trick up your sleeve just as I was taking off. So to make sure that doesn't happen . . ." he held up his free hand (the one that wasn't holding the knife to Paulo's neck) and revealed some metal chains he had found in the Train. "Move," he said.

"Come along, Evelyn," said the Captain.

Evie joined him. Mallory then walked over to them and with the knife constantly at Paulo's neck, forced them all to approach the old, disused cistern.

The ground under foot was rocky and uneven and the closer they got, Evie, Paulo and the Captain could see further down into the inky blackness of the hole. There were stony steps downwards, and then a sharp decline, where dusty rocks and pebbles rolled under foot as they were stepped on.

It was cold and damp inside. There was a noticeable change in the air. It was musty and stifled, and all four of them immediately noticed it was a little bit harder to breath. All Evie wanted to do was get out.

Mallory quickly set to work binding them up to the wall of the cistern. Luckily for him, there were built in 'safety' handles—put there so that in case anyone ever got trapped in the cistern, they would be able to hold themselves up above the water until someone realised they were down there. What was a safety precaution was to become their doom.

Soon, they were trapped. Evie, then Paulo, then the Captain—all in a row.

"And I suppose *this* is how you recalled the Train back into time and space just then eh, Captain?" Mallory said, confiscating the Link-Chip from his pocket. "We can't have you keeping that now can we?"

"That Radio-Link Chip is useless to you, Mallory," said the Captain from his chains. "It's programmed to work for me and me only." He was bluffing a little.

Mallory shrugged. "No matter, as long as you don't have it I'm happy." With that, he dropped it on the ground right in front of the Captain and stomped his heel down hard on it, squashing it into pieces. "Well, that's you out of the way. I best be on my way. The builders are probably arriving at any moment. I bet they're going to fill this old cistern in so that they can build on it. Probably why they've got all that cement made up and ready to use out there."

"But you've got what you wanted," said Paulo with hatred, "why trap us in here?"

"I told you. So I know you're not going to do anything clever while I take off. Also, because perhaps I'm a bit of a meanie as well."

"What's to stop us from yelling and shouting and getting those workers to hear us and rescue us?" said Evie.

"Mmm," he said in mock-thought. "Perhaps this." He suddenly pulled out a little vile of clear fluid. On the top was a nozzle—like on a perfume bottle. He quickly sprayed one cloud of the stuff into each of their faces and within seconds, each one of them fell asleep. Mallory stepped back and looked at them, putting the bottle back in his pocket. "Sweet dreams," he said and climbed back up the slope out of sight.

While the three of them stood there sleeping, there was a *chuff choofety chuffing* that grew louder and then slowly faded. Slowly faded out of space and time. Mallory had finally broken free of that primitive ancient world.

Chapter Twenty-One

Pockets

Mum was on her way back to Evie's bedroom with a big bowl of hot water. She'd just taken off her socks and saw that mum had filled the bowl with suds as well. Evie's heart was full of gratitude. This was the good part about being sick—being taken care of by mum, 5-star service. She slid her feet down blissfully into the bowl, feeling like her whole body could melt into it. She felt restful, happy and warm. But when she turned her head to watch mum walk back down the hallway, the water grew cold. The hallway was longer than usual. Mum never came to its end, she just kept walking straight and the image of her kept fading more and more into the distance—a foggy blackness. By the time she could no longer see her, the water was stone cold. Evie called out to mum for another top up with fresh, hot water, but her voice wouldn't come. She tried lifting her feet out of the water but found she couldn't move them. The water had thickened and started sticking around her feet. She looked down at them and felt a shock run through her. The water had turned into browny-grey muck, and there were veins, no—roots, climbing up her legs with alarming speed. She tried to stand up from her bed, but this only made it worse. The roots, having taken hold of her calves, began to pull her down. She felt them sucking her down into the bowl of muck below—always moving downwards slowly, but never reaching the bottom.

Then, she sensed herself waking up from a dream, and remembered suddenly where she was. On instinct, she looked down at her feet and with the little light there was, she was terrified to see that her feet were indeed completely covered by muck. A cold and sticky mixture of rocky dirt, water, ash and what looked like bits of straw and goodness knows what else. She could hear voices of men a little distance away, and the grating and churning of primitive machinery. She panicked and tried immediately to wake the other two up. Paulo was right next to her, and the Captain right next to him. When she called their names, she knew that some kind of cloth had been pulled tightly across her mouth. When she turned her head to see the others, they too had been gagged. With all the body movement she could manage, she nudged Paulo and yelled as best she could in his ear.

Despite her not being very loud, he did wake up slowly, blinking his eyes and then going through the same panic that she did only a minute ago.

By shaking her head this way and that, Evie managed to loosen the gag a little. "Wake up the Captain, we've got to get out of here!" she said.

Paulo loosened his gag as well. "What happened?"

"I don't know, we fell asleep somehow and now they've started working up there."

"Marius must be miles away by now," said Paulo.

"Light years, you mean."

"What are we going to do without the Train?"

"I don't know. But one thing I do know is that the Captain's gone mad. He practically handed the Train over to him gift wrapped!"

"And now we're going to be drowned in . . . what is this stuff anyway?"

"Cement. The ancient formula. You know, the old quicklime, pozzolana and pumice." It wasn't Evie's voice. It was the Captains'.

"Captain! You're awake," said Evie.

"Yes, and I heard you use the 'm' word when referring to me."

"What, *mad*? Well you are!"

"No need for flattery. What seems to be the trouble?"

"Are you still asleep?" said Evie. "Look around. We're going to be buried alive! That's what the trouble is."

"Yes, I'll admit it's quite a sticky situation."

"Are you trying to be funny?" said Paulo.

"Although I have to say, it's quite interesting as well."

"Interesting?"

"To actually witness the building methods of Bible times. I'd say they're using some sort of gutter-like structure to pour in all that cement. They were clever back in these times, you know. They managed quite a lot without computers and machines and robots. Mind you, they did have to work harder. However, they probably don't suffer from the stress we experience when our computer packs up."

Evie was wondering how she ever managed to trust the Captain. He appeared now to have (as the saying goes) flipped his lid. She called out as loud as she could, "HELP!!!"

Paulo joined her for the second time, "HELP!!!!!!"

"Captain, help," said Paulo. "Someone's bound to hear us."

So he did help, for the third attempt. "HELP!!!!!!!!!!!!!!!!!!!!!!!!"

No one appeared to hear them. All that happened was this: the end of a gutter-like structure showed itself at the opening of the cistern and down it, poured a long, thick, gluggy stream of cement, and the three prisoners could feel the cold, wet substance as it formed a new surface level around their calves.

"Why can't anyone hear us?" said Evie, growing more and more fearful.

"This underground hole absorbs a lot of sound," said the Captain, "and the men working up there are not right on top of us. They could be some distance away with other jobs. Mixing the cement, flattening the ground . . ."

"And what about the Train?" Evie said, almost angry at him.

"Ah yes, well I was going to explain about that, you see . . ."

Another big load of cement came slopping down into the hole.

"Never mind that now," said Paulo, "we've got to think of a way of getting out of here first!"

The thick mud rested up below their knees.

"First thing," the Captain said, "keep your legs moving. This cement won't set as quickly as the cement you're familiar with, but best to keep moving anyhow."

"Is there are a second thing?" said Evie.

"Erm . . . turn out your pockets."

Paulo went to do as he'd said, but . . . "We can't, our hands are tied up."

"Oh yes. Well, can you remember what's in your pockets at this moment? Let's list their contents and decide if any of it will be useful."

"Okay."

"Evelyn?" asked the Captain.

"Um . . . a hair tie I think, and . . . there'd be that tissue I used the other day."

"O . . . kay, not a good start. Paulo?"

"My lock pick that I used to get inside the Train . . ."

"I should confiscate that, you rascal." He sighed, "But what a pity these aren't hand cuffs instead of chains. Pick the locks in them—easy. Anyway, go on."

"Er . . . I have a small spanner and a screwdriver. A piece of fruit from the valley."

"Ooo," said the Captain, giving the others a glimpse of hope.

"What, you reckon the acidity of the fruit could eat through the chains?"

"No, I reckon we could eat it. I'm starving, aren't you?" The Captain paused in thought. "Anything else?"

"Not that I can think of. What have you got, Captain?"

"Yeah, you seem to carry around a whole hardware and electronics shop constantly in your pockets, Captain," said Evie. "Surely you'll have something good."

"Now let me see . . . a torch, the flat-top snake venom, my Portable Audio Clandestine Digital Communicators*, my Manual Hand Operating Fuel Injected Flame Combust . . . sorry—my lighter, the Atom Relocating Molecular Teleport Device if Mallory

---

* In other words, a pair of complex walky-talkies.

kept his word, my Dimensionally Versatile Ocular Portal Lens♣, the Vernacular Recognition and Decoding Box♦, an old tissue, a photograph, and that's all I can remember. Unfortunately, the Unique Radio-Wave Operated Link Chip is crushed to bits and buried somewhere under all this muck."

"So . . . anything useful out of all that?" Evie asked.

"Nnnnot really. You sure you don't have that whistle still on you, Evelyn?"♠

"No, I left it on the Train," she replied, realizing how annoyingly brilliant it would be if she still had it on her. It would capture anyone's attention in the whole area.

"So what are we going to do?"

Another huge load of cement came rushing down and sloshing uncomfortably around their knees.

"Captain?" Evie said urgently.

The Captain said nothing. His face showed a decline in confidence that luckily Paulo and Evie could not see in the poor light.

Portia was tired of waiting. She'd waited for what seemed like all day for her husband to return, and when he had, he'd ignored her. Now she didn't know whether to wait for him again or . . .

She realised there wasn't really an 'or'. What else *could* she do but wait? Her bizarre conversation with that slave girl, Evelyn—even though she did think it was all

---

♣   A gadget we have not yet had the pleasure of seeing in action.

♦   Possibly an explanation as to why Roman and Jewish people seem to have been speaking in English to the three travellers.

♠   The whistle that had come in very handy in their last adventure a couple of times.

nonsense—still made her uneasy. It made her realise that she'd never fully come to trust Marius. Not in the way a wife should be able to trust her husband.

The more she thought about it, the more uneasy she became. There was someone who understood finally. Understood what Marius was like. And now he wasn't coming home and there'd seemed to be such urgency in the way Evelyn and that man took off in the chariot. Was Marius in danger? . . . Was Marius himself, the danger?

After a quick impulsive decision, she left the house. She could ask around the village if anyone had seen him . . . or perhaps the girl and the man she'd called the Captain. While Portia ran outside, she almost collided with a big, shiny, brown horse—the one that had been left there by Marius and those two men when they'd whipped through like a violent wind. She smiled at her good fortune, and acquainted herself with the animal. She saw that its saddle was filthy dirty—and strangely, sticky with some sort of residue. Besides that, she noticed the reins were growing brittle and the horse was clearly becoming irritated by the heavy bags that were draped on either side of it. She unclipped the lot, and decided to re-saddle him. She knew that Marius' gear was much newer and more reliable, so she ran to the stable and plummeted through the doors, grabbing a new saddle and strong, hardy reins. When she lifted up a pile of blankets to take with her, a couple of crates were revealed with soil in them, and some kind of plant growing in them. Its leaves were huge, and when the blankets were lifted away, its thick stems had flopped over the side of the crates. She smelt it—not a strong scent, then felt its leaves—they were velvety, thick, and a little bit prickly.

How strange, she thought. She'd never seen a plant quite like it. And why would Marius have it here? She frowned in thought, but then shrugged, gathering up her supplies and hurrying back to the horse.

"You're a lovely fellow aren't you," she said, as she saddled him up. Soon, she was able to mount him and off she went. Off to ask the neighbours what had happened to her husband.

"Captain, do you have any sort of plan at all?" Evie said as she could feel the thick gravelly mud settling around her hips.

"Well, I might be able to think of some amazing and impressive escape plan using the objects in our pockets but . . ."

"You'd need an amazing and impressive plan to get *into* our pockets," said Paulo.

"Exactly. And . . ." he pulled and tugged and wriggled violently in his chains, ". . . there's nothing coming to mind." Behind his back however, the brittle, crumbling wall started to give, after his last fierce tug. His hands, although centimeters away from the wall, didn't feel the progress he'd just made, and so he drooped his head and believed that tugging at the wall would never do any good.

Chapter Twenty-Two

Commotion At The Inn

They never gave up yelling. That was one plan they always had up their sleeves—one that might even work if they did it at the right time. But I'm sorry to inform you—it didn't at this stage. Nobody heard them.

They kept on stomping their legs too. Marching, all three of them, in a row, underneath the sludge, and boy, were their legs getting tired. Every muscle in their legs was burning,* but they dare not stop.

---

* Because it wasn't like moving your legs through water. You try and march whilst half immersed in a pool of thick gluggy porridge. You probably know what it's like to move through water—a little bit harder than moving through air. That's because the tiny particles that make up water are closer together than the particles in the air, so it's harder to push through. Particles in solid objects, like a table, or a wall, or a number 47 bus are so close together, you cannot push through them, (which is why you don't generally see people walking through walls). The consistency of the thick sludgy cement that Evie, Paulo and the Captain were standing in at this moment was somewhere in between water, and a solid object . . . very hard work.

Evie had a horrible feeling, as the sludge climbed up to her tummy that she'd be marching like this for the rest of her life.

At an expensive, ritzy inn in a very Roman area of Jerusalem, there was a commotion that broke out suddenly. Horse hooves could be heard clopping loudly on the ground, the dust being kicked up in clouds all around it. Then came its loud, distressed neigh. Following this, there was a thud and a series of at-the-time unintelligible cries from a very exhausted and dishevelled woman. She picked her way through the busy street outside the inn, and as she staggered and pushed her way through the dense torrent of people. Members of the crowd when they caught glimpse of her would scream or gasp in sympathetic horror.

One cried out, "Get away from me!"

Another called, "Leper!"

Others were saying, "Don't let her touch you!"

Someone somewhere said, "Someone help her!"

She'd reached the entrance of the inn and reached out with her discoloured arm. She was indeed afflicted with some horrific disease.

The inn-keeper rushed to the door when he noticed the happenings outside, saw her there reaching out and said, "We're all full up here, I'm sorry!" and went to shut the door—shut her and whatever disease she carried with her out.

But she had already wedged her foot in the door and she was leaning against it, trying to get in.

"Please woman, I have nowhere for you to rest here."

"Please, I need help!" she said, desperately.

"I don't think there's anything I can do for you." He was obviously believing those who thought she had a terrible, catchy, deadly disease. And by this time, some of the inn-keeper's guests were standing around watching.

"Please," she persisted.

"I can't let you in here," he persisted.

"This is not leprosy*," she tried to tell to him. "Something is wrong with me but it is not that. I wonder if someone can help me."

"I don't think so. We have no physician here to . . ."

He was interrupted by a voice just behind him in the entrance of the inn, "Portia?" The person pushed his way through the curious, yet sickened onlookers and came up beside the inn-keeper. "It is you, Portia." He went to open the door, but the inn-keeper insisted on keeping lots of distance between himself and the woman.

The woman-Portia, recognised the man as Lucius, her brother-in-law.

"What has happened, Portia?"

"I do not know," she started to cry. "But I think I am dying."

Next, Camilla came beside Lucius and witnessed Portia's affliction as well. "Oh dear, Portia. For pity's sake, man, let her in," she said to the inn-keeper.

"If I do, I place everyone here—including myself—in great danger. We don't know what we could catch!"

Camilla broke past the man and her and Lucius went *outside* the inn and shut the door behind them.

♣   A highly contagious and fatal disease, which was common back in these times. Sufferers of it would be isolated from society and forced to live with other lepers so that they could not infect others.

"I know that it is not leprosy," repeated Portia to them.

"We can see that it is not. But what is it?"

The inn-keeper was watching through the window of his inn—from a distance.

"I . . . think it's . . . poison. I can feel something in my throat and in my stomach. Something is not right."

"Surely Cardea . . ." said Lucius, "if we call on Cardea . . ."

"Calling out for your supposed goddess of health won't do anything," came a new voice from around the side of the inn.

It was Levi, the Jewish slave.

"Levi, how dare you scoff the gods. Why is it do you think they do not choose to honour you?"

"The God I believe in is the God of health, land, sky, water, light; everything."

"Do you know what is wrong with Portia?"

"No, I've never seen anything like it. But I think you ought to take her to the Temple for prayer."♣

"The Temple of Jerusalem?"

Levi nodded.

The pair almost told him off for speaking so boldly to his masters and telling them what to do. But Portia was family. They were willing to try anything and they had no time to lose.

Lucius said, "His God is as good as any, come on."

♣ Back in these days, before Jesus died on the cross, to get within talking distance of God, you had to go to the temple where there were priests and where God's presence was.

Before they could go anywhere, the inn-keeper shouted from his window, "Hey, you need to pay for staying at my inn! You can't just run away like that!"

They stopped and looked at each other. Lucius and Camilla couldn't bring themselves to cheat the man, so among them they came up with a solution.

"Levi, you are to take Portia to the temple in the chariot, and have her prayed for. Do all you can, do you understand?"

"Yes."

"And return here as soon as possible to bring us news."

"Yes, of course." And he blasted into action, sitting Portia in the chariot, untroubled by her sickness and the possible consequences of being in contact with it. He pounded the horses into action and off he rode, leaving a thick cloud of dust behind him.

The cement was quickly reaching the Captain's ribcage. Because Paulo was a little bit shorter than him, it was settling around his chest. And because Evie was the shortest of them all, the cement was swirling around her shoulders!

Because of her panic, Evie had not been able to hold back her tears. "Captain *do* something! I'm scared!" In fact she had never been so scared in her life.

The Captain was scared too. He literally had no ideas of how to get them out of this. Oddly though, he had a funny way of showing his fear. He let out a sudden, confident and slightly hysterical laugh. "Don't you see what this means? No way at all of getting out of here?"

"Yes, it means we'll DIE!"

"No no no no no no no! I only want positive thinking at the moment please."

"I'm sorry, Captain but I can't think of anything positive at the moment."

"We have no way of escape, we're absolutely helpless, which means, we have to rely totally on God! If He gets us out of this situation . . . which He will," he added optimistically, "then we can't say it was anything *we* did! It'll be a full-sized, no-doubt, utterly-pure miracle! It'll make a fan*tastic* story to tell!"

"Aren't you scared though?"

The Captain was of course scared. But he was excited too. He said in his head, "Get us out of here please God, I'm not ready to die just yet." Then he said with a certain gleam in his eye, "What amazing thing do You have planned, I wonder?"

Evie wished she could have the Captain's confidence. Sure, she believed in God. But miracles like what the Captain was expecting now, only happened in Bible times! Things like Moses parting the Red Sea, and Jesus raising people from the dead. She'd never seen miracles like that happen in her own life. This, however, didn't stop her hoping and praying. She wriggled her hands in the chains behind her back. She was terrified to feel that the consistency of the cement around the chains was very thick and sticky. She thought, surely, that with every minute passing, the cement was literally gluing itself to the chains and to the wall behind her. She felt sick.

"The Temple!" Levi called over his shoulder to Portia, "I can see it! We'll be there soon." Then he spoke quieter, "Lord Father, have mercy on this woman. She does not know you as her God yet, but please let us get to the Temple in time so that You may be glorified!" He suddenly realised Portia hadn't answered him before. "Mistress?! Are you awake?"

There was a grunt from the back, followed by a choking sound—as if she was trying to speak but couldn't for all the gunk in her throat.

"Just stay awake Mistress, don't give up! We're nearly there!"

When the horses were approaching the vicinity of the Temple, Levi was forced to slow down. There was a Roman soldier in front of him, responsible for the hold up. Behind him, was a big busy mess of workers, building equipment, piles of dirt, mud and straw, and all sorts of digging and building tools.

"Where do you want to go?" asked the Roman.

"The Temple. It is very urgent! Please say I can get there!"

"You can get there. But you have to go around. Can you not see, there is a building project in progress here? By order of King Herod."

Levi felt frustrated, but he took a breath and hurriedly got the horses moving again. Having to travel around the whole building area was going to take longer than riding to the temple in a straight line, but he wasn't going to give up.

He soon found a clear way around. The horse was being pushed to gallop at top speed. The ride was so bumpy; Portia and Levi were being thrown a good height into the air with every stride. And although it seemed to be a large detour, Levi never lost sight of the big and beautiful Temple ahead of them.

As the cement was levelling around her neck, Evie's breathing became faster and faster; she could not control it. She wondered if this was what a panic attack was like. As an automatic reaction, she cried out as loud as she could, and with it, she heard herself choking up, beginning to cry.

"Stay calm, Evie," said the Captain, "everything's going to be alright!"

"That's easier for you to say, you're only in up to your shoulders!"

"Keep yanking on the chains. They might give!"

"I think my chains are cemented to the wall, Captain," said Paulo.

Paulo felt it crawling up his neck, and Evie cried out again for help when she felt it touch her chin.

These are my last moments, she thought. *Mum'll never know what happened to me. Dad'll probably talk about that time I spilt milk all over him at my funeral service. And James . . . James'll probably think I died way back on Satellite SB-17.*

"Arrghhh!" cried the Captain, all of a sudden. "My hands are free!"

"Quick, get us out!" shouted Evie, absolutely bawling, exploding with tears.

The Captain took a step towards his friends as quick as he could.* But when his foot landed on the ground beneath him, it slid with an unexpected jerk and his leg gave way underneath him. Evie screamed when she saw the Captain's head disappear underneath the surface of cement.

"Captain!" Paulo exclaimed. He hadn't stopped yanking on his own chains. "Captain get up!" he yelled

---

*   which was extremely slow, given the thickness of the cement.

encouragingly, even though the Captain probably could not hear him under there.

There was movement under the surface and next thing, the Captain's head emerged again—unrecognisable. He wiped away the cement from his mouth and eyes and waded carefully over to Evie. She was the priority, since she was the closest one to being completely submerged.

He pushed his hand through the thick muck, around her waist and found her hands. He noticed her legs weren't moving anymore. "Evie, keep moving!"

"I can't, when I move, it makes my head bob up and down. I don't really want to taste this stuff."

There was no time to waste. Any second, there could be another big load of cement sloshing down that gutter, and that would be the load that smothers them all.

Evie was terrified and she whimpered, "Get them undone, Captain, I want to get out of here."

The Captain, with a determined face, feeling his way round the chains, couldn't bear hearing Evie's voice—so frightened. It was because of him that she was going through this. And Paulo for that matter. Although Paulo was trying to hold it together, he was just as terrified as Evie.

As the Captain fingered the knot of chains behind Evie's back, he felt a burning hot stirring in his stomach as his impatience for the chains welled up.

His face being so close to her's, Evie could hear him muttering under his breath, until that name again came darting out of his mouth. "Jesus!"

Then in a second, both the Captain and Evie felt the chains loosening, as if the name, like a bullet, had blown them apart.

"Now Paulo," said the Captain. And at that very moment, they could hear another load rolling down the gutter and slopping down into what was now a giant, underground, cement lake.

"No!" the Captain yelled, just as he saw both Paulo and Evie taking a deep breath, preparing to go under. "Evie, get out! We'll be right behind you!"

She found it hard to leave. For two reasons. One: she wanted to make sure the Captain and Paulo were going to be able to leave as well; and two: she could find no foothold, nothing to get a grip onto to heave herself out to safety. Every time she took a step, the ground was deeper than she expected and her body always plummeted forward, leaving her arms thrashing around, trying to grab onto the wall to steady herself. It was like every time she took a step forward, a force was dragging her back and no matter how hard she tried, that light in the entrance was getting no nearer at all.

Chapter Twenty-Three

The Lethal Lake

"I can't get out!" she cried.

"I can't loosen Paulo's chains!" the Captain replied.

"Hello?!!" Another voice cried . . . "Is anyone down there?!"

Evie couldn't believe it. "Yes!!" she practically screamed. "Yes! Down here!" She could hear running footsteps coming towards the cistern, but it wasn't for a few seconds that she saw someone—two people. One teenaged boy and a young woman dragging herself along behind him.

"What happened?" she heard the boy say.

Evie could not see properly for the dirt and mud in her eyes. "Just help us, please! There's three of us!"

Whoever he was, he wasn't afraid of getting dirty. He hopped straight in and immediately saw the man behind Evie struggling to get a third person free. Not realising Evie's own struggle to get out, he headed straight for the Captain.

The Captain briefed the newcomer, "I'm trying to get the chains undone. It's what's holding him to the wall."

"I'll do that, you keep his head above the surface."

And that's what they did. The Captain held his hand under Paulo's chin and said to him with urgency. "Paulo, are you still with me?"

Paulo nodded his head. "Are we going to be alright?"

"I believe so, but we're not out of the woods yet."

"You mean we're not out of the cement yet, Captain. Have you started to hallucinate?"

The Captain couldn't help smiling. *

Evie was stumbling and fumbling around. She had found the wall and was now trying to walk along it, but now that another load had been dropped in there, she could not touch the bottom without dunking her head under a little bit. She was taken back to when she was about eleven. She thought she could look pretty cool going into the deep end of the swimming pool at her friend's birthday party, but she only ended up panicking and feeling those horrible jumpy butterflies in her stomach, and being sure for at least a few seconds that she was going to drown.

Splosh! She lost her footing and was now buried well under the surface. She flapped her arms and legs like a person insane but it was useless. No amount of pushing or paddling got her anywhere near the surface again.

Until, something grabbed her hand, and then her arm. At first, she had a grave feeling it was tugging her further downwards. But then, with one smooth motion, she was dragged along, through the mud pit. Shortly, she

---

* Just so you know, 'not out of the woods yet' is an expression people use to explain that there might be a glimmer of hope, but they're not completely out of trouble yet. Paulo was not familiar with the expression, having been born on another planet.

found she could breathe again. Then next thing, she was out, and she had never felt so free!

"That's got it!" the boy said suddenly, and the Captain immediately started dragging Paulo towards the entrance of the cistern. The boy helped to push him along, but he found it very hard, as he was no taller than Paulo. The Captain was almost pulling both of them along.

Evie had landed on someone—presumedly the person who had pulled her out. She wiped the cement away from her eyes and saw the woman who'd followed the boy down here. She frowned in amazement. "Portia?" Portia herself could not speak. She just curled over, weak and frail, and coughed and coughed and coughed into the ground. "What's wrong?"

The three others were crawling out of the pit and up the old stone wet-cement-covered steps. They looked like horrible undead monsters rising up out of a stagnant, sludgy, mucky swamp. When the boy spoke, Evie recognised him as Levi.

"Portia needs help too," he said, breathlessly. "She can't breathe properly and she has a terrible kind of rash spreading. I was on my way to the Temple to pray for her."

"Sounds like the state Silius was in," said the Captain, also short of breath.

Paulo had climbed out and drew himself next to the woman, wiping his face with his hands. He saw her skin, her coughing. "It is, Captain. It's the Violet Assassin. She looks terrible. She might be too far gone."

"Be positive. You still got that fruit in your pocket?"

"Yes!" Paulo said, hoping it wasn't covered in cement or squashed to a pulp and all the juice gone.

He pulled it out, and because Paulo's overall pockets were quite deep,* the fruit was unharmed. "Here," he said, giving Portia the fruit, "eat this, quick!"

Levi had still insisted they go to the Temple and it wasn't for the Captain to argue—he wanted to go there simply to see it! When the five of them approached, Evie felt like a tourist gazing up at it in the hot midday sun.

The Captain and Levi had said a prayer for Portia while they were still on their way, and Evie had kind of joined in. That is, she agreed with everything they'd said.

There were a lot of people around. People going up and coming down the steps of the Temple entrance, people lining up at a gate just within the Temple with money bags in their hands, and lots of people just generally walking past, going about their business. It looked like the place to be—the central focal point of Jerusalem. When they reached the entrance of the Temple, Levi—with Portia clinging on to him, using his strong young body as a crutch—headed straight into the big beautiful entrance. The Captain followed. An opportunity to see the Temple of Jerusalem in its glory was too good to miss. So naturally, Evie and Paulo followed as well. They sensed people staring at them and giving them funny looks. They weren't to be blamed, however. The small group did look quite ridiculous. Four covered in thick undeterminable muck, and one with an ugly, unknown skin condition.

Directly inside the massive temple wall, was a spacious courtyard paved with colourful cobble stone. Evie and

---

* Although, not quite as deep as the Captain's.

Paulo were looking around in wonder. Evie had been told a little bit about the Temple of Jerusalem at church and seen diagrams of it in the back of her Bible, but she never dreamt it would be so huge or so beautiful. Paulo, on the other hand, had never seen it, or heard about it. *

They didn't get much of a chance to stick around and admire it though; Levi took Portia straight through to a big, beautiful gate ◆ and entered.

When the Captain, Paulo and Evie followed, they were stopped in their tracks—first by Levi himself, and then a priestly looking fellow who wore long, expensive robes.

"You can not come any further," said Levi, politely to the three of them. "I don't think you are Jewish, are you?"

The three looked at each other. Paulo and Evie didn't know what to say, so the Captain answered. "Well, no, we're not."

Then Levi looked at Portia, "I will go on ahead and pray on behalf of you."

"But why should your god, the God of the Israelites extent his protection over me—a Roman?"

"My God is a God of mercy and His mercy is not limited to His people only. Have you heard the stories about Rahab and Ruth? They were ancestors of King David, yet they were not Israelites and God poured out mercy on them."

"I have not heard," sighed Portia, sounding like she had pebbles in her throat. "But I trust that they are true.

---

*   They don't go into this in 'Interplanetary Studies' at school on Serothia.

◆   Believe it or not, the gate was actually called 'Gate Beautiful'.

If there is such a God as merciful as yours, I want to know Him and be counted as one of His."

Levi gave all of them a polite smile and continued on through the Temple.

"Can't Portia even go any further in?" Evie asked the Captain.

The Captain explained to her and Paulo that this courtyard they were standing in now was the 'Court of the Gentiles'. Anyone who wasn't a Jew was called a Gentile and weren't allowed to go beyond that point.

"The next chamber is called the 'Court of Women'," explained the Captain, "Levi could take her there if she was an Israelite. But he'll go further in, do some prayer, make an offering, stuff like that."

"Does the 'Court of Women' mean that women aren't allowed to go any further?" Evie asked, completely confused.

"Bingo," said the Captain. "It's a very different world from what you're use to. Women were looked on as much lower than men in these times."

Evie felt a little disgusted by this, and looked as though she was about ready to begin a women's revolution two thousand years early. But she contained herself, remembering that where she came from, there was a female Pastor at her friend's church. Not to mention, a female Prime Minister.

"Captain, I know you probably haven't forgotten," said Paulo out of the blue, but quietly so that Portia wouldn't hear, "but after all this, we still don't have the Train. You act as though everything's okay again but, well didn't Mallory just take off with it. He could be anywhere in the entire universe by now! What are we going to do?"

"Or is this our new home, Captain?" asked Evie, trying to stay patient with him.

All the Captain did was raise his eyebrows as if he'd just remembered something exciting, and said, "Ah!"

Portia was gaining strength all the time, and it was arranged that for now, Portia would stay at the inn where Lucius and Camilla were staying. They had all ridden the chariot there already, and washed off the worst of the cement.

The Captain tried to explain all he could to Portia in a way she could understand about Marius—the man who was her husband. "From what I can gather, he was stranded here by a former friend. He wasn't from this world so he had to learn this culture fast and blend in. He met you . . . and I don't know whether he genuinely fell in love and decided it would be a good way of blending in . . . or . . . whether he only thought it would be a good way to blend in. As soon as a way opened up for him to get out, he took the opportunity."

"Without even saying goodbye." Evie felt sad for Portia and the situation she now found herself in. She was so angry at the man for doing that to this lady—who really was rather sweet. "You'll be alright, won't you?"

"I do not know," she said, her eyes desolate. "I do not even have a slave anymore . . . for company if nothing else."

Levi said, "Perhaps Lucius will arrange something, Mistress."

"Perhaps." She looked up at Levi. "Thank your god for me. He is yet another god of health that must be remembered."

"He's the God of everything," Levi said. He didn't have the nerve to add 'He is the only, one true God'.

"Well, we must leave now," said the Captain, grabbing hold of the reins on that trusty, hardworking horse that Portia had ridden there. He mounted, and then gestured to Paulo and Evie to hop on as well.

"Three people can't get on there!" said Evie.

"Who says? You can do it, can't you old boy!" he said, patting the neck of the horse. "Yes, you're a good boy! Anyway, it won't be for long. We'll pick up Elisha's other horse from the palace on our way."

"On our way where?"

There was no answer yet from the Captain. Before he got on the horse, however, he reached into his pocket and pulled out the bottle of yellow fluid. "Levi, there's something important I need you to do. And you'll probably need lots of help." With the help of Paulo and Evie as well, he explained about the Violet Assassin. There were many unanswered questions and mysteries for Levi. Deep down he didn't understand it, but he trusted Evie, and therefore, he trusted the Captain. He said, "I would do as you say; only I am not free to make my own decisions."

Portia then butted in, "I will do this thing with Levi. No one must suffer what I suffered." She took the bottle from him. "You say just a small drop?"

"A *tiny* drop."

"You can rely on us, Captain," said Levi.

With Levi's help, Paulo got on the horse behind the Captain, and Evie squeezed on behind Paulo, feeling like she was going to slip off the back at any moment.

"Thank you for saving our lives!" the Captain said to Levi and Portia. Then he spoke specifically to Levi, "You're a good soldier."

"Soldier?"

"For the only battle worth fighting. Keep trusting in the One and Only." He winked and then commanded the horse to get a move on. "Adios!" And the horse galloped away like a bullet, leaving a wake of dust behind him.

"Faster, faster, faster!" shouted the Captain, almost like a little child getting a piggy-back ride on his dad.

"Slower, slower, slower!" cried Evie, feeling terribly unsafe.

"Sorry Evelyn, you're going to have to hold on!"

And with that, the horse accelerated even more.

As for Mallory, he too, was accelerating. With sweat beading off his forehead, he darted around the Train's engine room, figuring out ways of disappearing out of the solar system—out of the galaxy, faster, faster.

Chapter Twenty-Four

Breaking Free

Two horses were now galloping side by side across the wide open plains of Judea. Majestic in every movement, they charged powerfully over the terrain like a well-oiled machine. Their hooves pounding into the earth, their robust form working with such ease and magnificence, while their manes flapped gracefully in the swift passing breeze.

The riders upon their backs were determined and having the ride of their lives. Paulo was riding one horse, and the Captain was riding the other, with Evie holding on for dear life on the back.

Evie's body was buzzing with excitement—not to mention the adrenalin. Even though it was a terrifying and turbulent ride, she'd never felt this way before. Her lungs were gaping for air. Even though she was breathing in so much of it, it never seemed to be enough. She had a smile from ear to ear and when she looked over to Paulo, she could see he had the same emotion. It was that funny mix of terror and fear, with joy and ecstasy and it's like your face isn't quite sure how to exhibit it.

There was yet another emotion in Evie and Paulo that I haven't mentioned yet. And that was bewilderment. They were completely in the dark about what they were doing and where they were going. Only the Captain seemed to know. Whatever it was, the Captain obviously felt it was too urgent to waste time talking about. By looking at him, one could sense that every second was vital.

"Where are we going?!" Evie shouted above the sound of the wind howling in her ears.

"We're going to where all this started!" he called back. "We're going to get the Train back!"

Evie didn't know whether this was a statement of what was going to happen next, or more like hopeful, positive thinking. Whatever it was, it filled her and Paulo with hope too.

The scenery had started to change after a while. There were more and more palm trees and a couple of roads here and there. The travellers were drawing nearer to Bethlehem. It was just reaching dusk and they could smell scents wafting from the town. Smoke from camp fires and wood stoves, fresh bread and herbs, the warm comforting aroma of home cooking.

But as they were approaching the town, the Captain surprised the other two by galloping straight past, not losing any speed.

Right back to where it started, thought Evie, *the hills and field where the Train landed—of course.* But then she tried to think of what possible good would that do.

The air was cooling. They wished they still had their brand new robes from Bethlehem now, instead of either using them as a bag to carry the Violet Assassin, or losing it to the angry-faced Marius.

The horses galloped up a number of steep hills with their impressively muscular structure. When they were climbing upwards, the riders would lean forward to help them. When they came back down, they would lean back so as to even out the weight distribution.*

The Captain suddenly stopped where he thought the Train had landed, those few nights ago. That historic night. The birth of Salvation. He had not known then, that his landing there, was the birth of someone else's salvation. Freedom from an eight-year prison in ancient Jerusalem.

The Captain's horse came to a halt, and so Paulo stopped his as well. Giving the horse a generous pat on the neck, the Captain dismounted and walked around the area.

"I don't get it," said Evie, struggling to dismount herself. "What do you expect to find here?"

"At this moment, I'm looking for the Train."

"Train tracks?"

"No, the Train itself."

"Okay," said Evie, "I'll humour you," and she started looking, (almost in mock, as if she was pretending to look for something in front of a group of very young school children.)

"Here," said the Captain, handing her his old-school driving goggles. "Wear these. You know that the Train can't be seen with the naked eye."

"But it was stolen by Marius and his wacky space-age machine, remember? Are you losing your mind?"

The Captain gave her a look out the corner of his eye, as if to say *that hurt*, and *I wish you had some more faith in me*, at the same time. He slid his own pair of glasses onto his face.

---

* As any horse trainer (who knows their stuff) will tell you to do.

She put the goggles on. She felt stupid, but she did it. And both her and Paulo followed him around over the hills and valleys.

"What's supposed to have happened?" asked Paulo, wide-eyed and fascinated.

"When I got back from my mission to get the yellow-venomed flat-top snake's venom, as a precaution, I put a lock on the Train's controls . . ."

Evie breathed relief, "Why didn't you say so?"

"Don't get too relaxed," he said quickly, holding up a hand to her. "The lock hasn't always worked. In the past, it's simply not functioned properly, or people have tried to 'pick the lock' in a manner of speaking." He tossed a glance to Paulo.

A little later, after some minutes of searching, the Captain noticed that his companions were still very confused. He breathed in and out slowly and thought he could probably do them the courtesy of a proper explanation. Putting himself in their shoes for a moment, he realised they deserved it.

"The lock on the Train's controls isn't just a lock that will stop Mallory from moving anywhere."

"Like a steering lock in a car?" said Evie.

"Kind of," he said, pointing at her. "Well it's not one of those. It's a lock that will automatically activate when it does not recognise the driver."

"The Train can *recognise* people?" exclaimed Paulo.

". . . It's a very clever Train." There was a much more complex explanation, which the Captain didn't have time for now. "As a . . . kind of defense mechanism, the Train will jump back in space and time to the place and time it last made a journey from."

Evie comprehended. "But what are we doing *here*? That would be Marius' house!"

"And why didn't it activate when I brought Mallory and Silius in there?" asked Paulo.

"Well all I can guess is that you were the first to touch the controls. It recognised you and so relaxed its security. If at any time it responded to Mallory's presence there, the controls were overridden by me anyway when I brought you back to Earth at that construction site." He was speaking faster and faster. "The only thing I'm worried about is whether or not the Train, in all its cleverness, counted the journey from here to Mallory's house a few days ago. That one wasn't technically a journey. The Train's controls weren't engaged, it was merely being pulled by an external force out of the vortex and brought back into that room underneath the house."

Evie stared at him blankly. "I don't get it."

"I do," said Paulo, walking over to join the Captain. "You're saying the Train might think that its last journey was from *my* home to here."

"You mean the Train could be on Serothia?"

"In 2011," the Captain added.

Evie stood there with her mouth wide open.

"Use the link-chip," said Paulo eagerly. "You know, the thing you used to track down the Train. The thing that . . . Mallory destroyed." Paulo's face lost all eagerness suddenly.

"It'd be half-set in cement underneath Jerusalem by now," said the Captain.

". . . What are we going to do?"

"Wait. And pray."

"To this . . . 'God' of yours? A mere baby? What can he do?"

"Well, God isn't a baby . . . sort of." Evie had a vague understanding that Jesus was the same person as God. And trying to stay on the positive side for once, she said to Paulo, "He once turned an ocean into dry land so His people could escape from slavery." ♣

"What?" Paulo said, completely confused.

But then, at that moment, as they were approaching the top of another hill, Evie stopped dead in her tracks, staring straight ahead of her. "I can't believe it," she said softly.

The Captain and Paulo followed her gaze. Paulo didn't know what she had seen, but the Captain's face lit up immensely, a wide grin spread from ear to ear.

"Yes!" he exclaimed, and then ran across the hillside. Evie and Paulo looked at each other and then ran after him. Evie passed him the goggles and putting them on, Paulo saw straight away, that they were running towards the Train.

The Captain had stopped at the door and opened it with a key. When the other two reached his side, he grabbed them by the shoulder and turned them away quickly. "Don't look!" he shouted. "Wait here."

The Captain stepped up into the carriage room of the Train. It wasn't a pleasant sight.

Mallory was slumped in one of the chairs, he looked weak, pale and absolutely exhausted.

On the floor, between the engine room and the carriage room, lay the body of Silius—still and cold.

♣ You can read about this story in the book of Exodus in the Bible—chapter 4, verse 18 to chapter 15. The part about crossing the ocean is in chapter 13.

"You took your time getting here," Mallory said with a weak and croaky voice.

"Sorry, I would have gotten here sooner, only some lunatic chained my friends and I down in a cistern leaving us to be buried alive in cement."

Mallory's eyes closed, and he frowned as if in pain. "Water," he rasped.

The Captain reached inside one of his pockets and pulled out a small canteen of drinking water, knelt down beside Mallory and gave him a drink.

He took big gulps, spilling it all down his chin and neck. Then he stopped for air. "Why should you show me kindness?"

"I'm not showing you any kindness. It's only humane to give someone water when they're thirsty."

"Always the goody-two-shoes aren't you."

The Captain frowned and reiterated a question he'd asked before. "How do you know me?"

He smiled a wicked and almost teasing grin. "Just following the leader."

The Captain only frowned more, not knowing what the man was talking about.

"That boy with you . . . Paulo. With the blue overalls. He's somebody special I think."

"Everybody's somebody special."

"No but . . . he has no idea yet, does he?"

The Captain frowned harder. "About what?"

A sly smile crept onto Mallory's lips. "His overalls are like the sky. And so his time runs short."

There was a moment's silence. The Captain considered that perhaps Mallory was delirious from dehydration. "Come on," he said, trying to forget his nonsense. "Get up. We're going to give this poor man a respectful burial service and then I'm going to take you somewhere you can't cause any more trouble."

"But isn't that just giving him what he wanted?" Evie asked later on, when they were on their way back to the Train again. The Captain and Evie were leading, and Paulo had Mallory in custody a few paces behind.

"He can't stay here, he'll only try and conquer the world and mess things up."

"Where are you going to take him?"

The Captain paused before replying. "Back to his home. The government there can decide what to do with him."

"Which is?"

". . . Same place I'm from."

Evie gasped and looked excited. "You mean I'm going to find out where you come from? I'm going to see your home?"

"In reply to the first statement . . . it would seem so," (he didn't sound very enthusiastic about it), "and in reply to the second statement . . . my Train is more like home to me now. So really, you've already seen it. Before we do that though, we have to return some valuable property to Elisha and his family."

The Captain and Evie awkwardly maneuvered the two horses *inside* the humble little Train and seeing Elisha and his wife, Rachel, Noam and Jared and Miriam again was nice—even though they were all still mourning the horrific loss of the baby, Joshua.

It was difficult for them to leave again, but when they did all step inside the Train again, Mallory constantly glowering, the Captain fired up the controls. Paulo, as instructed by the Captain, had tied Mallory up in the carriage room while they had returned the horses. He had to ignore the man's many attempts at scoffing him and putting him down. The man even tried convincing him that perhaps the Captain was the bad guy in all this. He was the one doing the kidnapping now. He was making god-like decisions about Mallory's fate. Paulo tried not to listen.

Meanwhile, Evie was trying to make sense of the situation in the engine room. "So, the Train went back in time as well as back to the fields where it landed three nights ago?"

"Yes."

"So do you mean Marius . . . *Mallory*, has been sitting in here for all that time. All the time we met those shepherds, while we were with Rachel and her family, when I was arrested and even when I was with him as his slave?"

"A-huh."

"So, he was in two places at once?"

"A-huh."

"But wait a minute. If the Train has been sitting here since we left it three nights ago, why did we think it was missing in the first place? In the scheme of things, it's been here all the time. Why didn't we see it?"

"Because when we arrived here, it was stolen as soon as we stepped out. None of the last few days had happened yet. We changed a little piece of history. It happens sometimes, you tend to get used to it."

"I still don't get it."

"Well put it this way. If the Train was here all along, we would've had no reason to go looking for it, no reason to go exploring through Bethlehem and Jerusalem. We would not have ended up at Mallory's house, Mallory would not have tried to drive the Train and so the Train could not have ended up being sent back in time to land here . . . it's a paradox in other words."

"Time travel boggles the mind," she said puffing out her cheeks.

He pointed at her and smiled, "That's it! Now you've got it." Then a thought came to him. "By the way, what was it you were going to tell me that night after we'd been to the stable? When we'd just fare-welled Zacchaeus and Joshua?"

"Oh," Evie was a little embarrassed. "I said I think I understand what it all has to do with me. The whole thing about Jesus dying."

"Yes?"

"It hit me when my tear dropped on the little Baby's face. That Bible verse about Him taking our sorrows or something."

"Yeah?"

"Well I kind of realised that I'd been imagining Jesus died for the sins of the world."

"He did."

"Yeah but . . . that means *me* too! He died for *me*, not just the whole world. Does that make sense?"

"Perfectly," he smiled.

"Like . . . when I feel sad and cry and that—it's like He feels sad and cries with me. Because He knows what it's like to be human!"

They had been in flight for only about ten minutes and the Captain had been all the time working the controls—just about every one of them—moving around to every nook and cranny there was of the engine room.

Next thing, he said, "Right, all I have to do now is . . ." He pulled on a lever and there was a jolt and a hissing sound. Then he raised his arm up and reached for a string hanging from the ceiling. This let out a loud whistle sound—*just* like a real steam train going *whoo whoooooo!* I think he did it just for fun.

The Captain then looked up at Evie with just his eyes. From this point on, he didn't look very excited. He was simply carrying out a task that he had to do but really didn't want to. "Come along then." He sidled past her and stepped into the carriage room.

"Home sweet home, Mallory," he said, gazing down at him.

Paulo tugged on his tanned, solid arm and Mallory stood up. He looked at the Captain with contempt,* and all together, the group proceeded to the door.

The Captain stepped out boldly onto a vast field of fresh grass and took in a deep breath of air. The others plodded down after him and looked around at their environment.

Paulo and Evie were very pleased with what they saw. It looked like a very pleasant place to be. Peaceful, clean, open and airy. They were high on a hill top—one of many, and it was all the same as far as the eye could see.

However, both Mallory and the Captain were frowning.

"Something's wrong," said the Captain. He trudged back into the Train, "don't let him out of your sight!" he commanded Paulo.

While the Captain was inside the Train, Evie wandered a little way around the soft, green grass, enjoying the

---

*   which means he didn't like him very much.

sunshine. Paulo kept a tight grip on Mallory. He never for one second took his eyes off of him, but in doing so, felt a slow, cold chill run down his back. Not only because Mallory was an extremely unpleasant person to look at, but also because there was the slightest hint of an evil and scheming smile, crawling its way onto his face again.

Shortly, the Captain emerged again from the Train, looking somewhat bothered and inconvenienced. "This isn't the right place."

"Of course it's the right place, it's *perfect*," said Evie, evidently dazed by the beauty of it.

Paulo came up to the Captain, "Did you enter in a wrong coordinate or something?"

"I'm sure I didn't. Unless when Mallory was in there for three whole days, he stuffed up some of the controls. I imagine he would have been pressing all sorts of buttons and messing things up. He would have been trying *anything* to get the Train to take him somewhere, or even just to get *out* of the Train."

"Do you think it can be fixed? I don't fancy being Mallory's travelling buddy for much longer."

The Captain looked back and forth, behind Paulo and around the field where they had landed. He saw Evie roaming around, looking out at the countryside, he saw the Train standing behind him, as he still had his glasses on . . . but . . .

"Where *is* Mallory?" he said, looking at Paulo in the eyes.

Paulo's stomach dropped and suddenly his heart raced. He whipped his head around, left, right, all around! Mallory had vanished. Paulo and the Captain quickly rushed inside the Train. There was no sign of him there either.

"Where's Mallory?" the Captain shouted to Evie. "Did you see him?"

"What? No. Haven't seen anyone."

"He must have done a runner!" Paulo said, feeling completely rotten inside. He was responsible for letting him free. "I'm sorry Captain, I only took my eyes off him for a second!"

"Well whatever this place is, he's stuck here. And we can't be responsible for him running off. Come on, we're going." On his way to the door of the Train, he called, "Evelyn, come on, let's go!"

There was no reply.

"Evie?" called Paulo.

They looked at each other and the Captain stepped down again from the Train to look around.

"You don't think Mallory . . ."

"No, look," said the Captain, relieved but slightly perplexed. "There she is."

"What's she doing?"

Evie was walking down the hill, taking slow, even steps and holding a flower.

"I don't know." The Captain took a step closer. "Evelyn!" he called, cupping his hands around his mouth.

There was no way she could have not heard him. But she kept on walking, like she was in some kind of trance.

"I'll go get her," said Paulo and took off with a jog down the hill.

The Captain started to follow him, but then something made him stop and call out, "Stop Paulo! Get away!"

Paulo's eyes widened with terrified alarm. They were both looking at a strange sort of glow, pulsating all around Evie's body. With every second, it was getting larger and larger and then there was an ear-piercing screeching sound.

Evie remained on her feet, seemingly unaffected by the phenomenon. But both the Captain and Paulo had to cover their ears and soon, they were on their knees, suffering painfully from the noise.

They managed to look up to where Evie was, and the energy around her was whizzing around faster and faster, until it became so bright, Paulo and the Captain could no longer look, or they could easily have been blinded! But Evie, remaining unaffected, kept walking forward, head straight and face—captivated. Something was drawing her near—willing her to keep walking . . .

"Today in the town of David, a Saviour has been born to you; He is Christ the Lord."—Luke 2:11

"He was despised and rejected by men—a man of sorrows, and familiar with suffering . . . But the fact is, it was our pains He carried, our disfigurements, all the things wrong with us . . . it was our sins that did that to Him, that ripped and tore and crushed him—our sins! He took the punishment and that made us whole. Through His bruises, we get healed."—Isaiah 53:3-5

"A bad motive can't achieve a good end. He whose tongue is deceitful falls into trouble."—Proverbs 17:20

"A fortune made by a lying tongue is a fleeting vapor and a deadly snare."—Proverbs 21:6

"The Birth Of Salvation" Facts

History

The year 4 B.C. is just an estimate of what year Jesus may have been born in. There is no way of knowing for sure due to a number of factors.

I've conducted some research of how life was at this time, but some things have come out of my imagination rather than out of text books to simply help in the telling and development of the story.

Ancient cement (used by the Romans) was made from three main ingredients: **quicklime**, which is also called calcium oxide and produced by heating up limestone (which is a type of rock); **pozzolana**, which is a fine, sandy, volcanic ash first discovered in Italy; and **pumice**, which is a volcanic rock formed when lava mixes with water—a solidified rocky lava. The chemical reaction created when these three ingredients are combined, is what results in the 'cement' substance.

King Herod the Great was what is called a 'client' king. Although he had Roman soldiers as an army, he was himself a Jew—not a Roman. Although he was king of Judea, he was still under the Roman Emperor (Augustus Caeser) as Jerusalem was under Rome—a more powerful country. Herod ruled Israel, but Rome ruled Herod, so to speak.

Herod the Great was famous for his architecture and building projects in Jerusalem. It was he who rebuilt the Temple again after it had been destroyed for the first time. Sometimes this Temple is referred to as Herod's Temple.

As it happens, he died in 4 B.C.

The Massacre of the Innocents is an event that Matthew (one of the apostles) gives an account of in his book in the Bible. Apparently, there is no other historical record supporting the claim that King Herod made such a decree. However, Bethlehem was a small village and so there probably weren't many male children under the age of two and therefore, not many deaths. This could explain why there's no record of the event. Herod was guilty of many brutal acts—some of them include killing his wife and two of his own sons! So it might not be a surprise to some that he could have been someone to make a decree as spoken of in Matthew. As for me, although I like to see a lot of evidence for something before I agree with it, when I read it in the Bible, I trust God and believe it.

The Temple of Jerusalem was built in 19 B.C. designed by King Herod the Great. In the scheme of things it was the second temple to be built in Jerusalem. It was huge and breathtakingly beautiful—about 500 metres long and 300 metres wide. It was destroyed by the Romans in 70 A.D., however there was a third temple that was built after that.

The Birth Of Jesus

I have tried to stay as close as possible to what can be understood of the Christmas story presented in the gospels of the Holy Bible. I based the 'Jesus' birth' sections of the story mainly on Luke's account. But not every detail will line up perfectly with either the gospel's accounts, historic accounts, or your own idea of how things took place.

The Universe

The three wise men that we sing about at Christmas time and who many of us had to colour in on Nativity Colour-In sheets in primary school, were astronomers and/or astrologers—(there was no difference between the two back in those times). They watched the sky for scientific and religious reasons. Certain shapes in the night sky (the way stars and planets were aligned) meant different things to them. One night they saw a sign which meant 'a new king' and this is what caused them to go to King Herod and ask him what it was all about. Astronomers and historians now, have tried to use their knowledge of the stars and their patterns to pinpoint the actual date of Jesus' birth.

The Captain's 'The Beatles' Quotes

"It's been a hard day's night" / "We should be sleeping like a log"
     from the song "A Hard Day's Night"

"Hello hello"
     from the song "Hello Goodbye"

"There's nothing you can see that isn't shown"
     from the song "All You Need Is Love"

"Here come old flat-top"
     from the song "Come Together"

"Life is very short and there's no time for fussing and fighting my friends"
     from the song "We Can Work It Out"